SHACKLED

Z. GEYER

Book Cover and Formatting by Aila Designs (www.ailadesigns.com)

Edited by Stuart Budgen

1st edition 2024

ISBN Hardcover: 979-8-9910064-0-8

ISBN Paperback: 979-8-9910064-1-5

DEDICATION

Dedicated to you, the reader. Take your part in breaking shackles, be it your own or others.

Table of Content

CHAPTER 1

BRUTAL BEGINNING

The halls of the Seelie Palace were deadly silent, lit only by the faint purple glimmer of enchanted sconces, as Prince Thazin moved through the darkness, the hem of his embroidered robes trailing against the polished marble floor. At the end of the corridor, he paused outside a decrepit wooden door one room past his own.

With a wave of his hand, the magical locks disengaged, and the prince stepped inside Nova's barren quarters, wrinkling his nose at the musty straw scent. His piercing emerald eyes fell upon the slight form of the enslaved girl huddled on her thin mattress, and she sat up, blue waves of hair spilling over her shoulders – such a pretty face for one of impure blood. Nova's copper eyes locked with Thazin's, every muscle tensing; the fear spread across her face a palpable sweetness to the prince's tongue.

"On your feet," the prince purred, a cruel smile curling his lips, as Nova obeyed wordlessly, rising to meet whatever cruel whims he had for her this humid eve. She had been enduring the prince's sick games her whole life long and she was used to it. As Thazin approached, Nova stared at the floor, swallowing down the urge to flee, wishing he would take her life with the crystal dagger at his hip and finally allow her to rest eternally.

Thazin snatched a handful of her matted hair, yanking her head back, as he pressed her face against the bars of her sole window, making her face the very Moon her mother worshipped. "Buwan has forsaken you," he snarled out, spit spraying against the back of her head, as his other hand ripped away her already tattered garments.

Nova fell limp against the bars, as the sound of his drawers hitting the ground echoed through her chambers; the cold iron bars sizzling against her cheek and the side of her forehead as she squeezed her eyes shut, attempting to block out everything he was about to unleash upon her.

Thazin's magic held her still, pinned against the bars, as one of his hands took hold of the curve of her hip. Tears ran down her cheeks from the corners of her eyes, as she tried to focus on the sounds of the crickets singing just beyond her window.

He thrust his hips, slamming into her, and Nova let out a whimper. She knew better than to scream; it would only encourage him to retrieve his tools of agony. His grip tightened in her hair, holding her in place, as the prince let out a satisfied groan, and his movements grew faster; spearing his shaft inside her repeatedly, and leaving her a gaping mess as always.

It was like this each night. He would take her roughly, sometimes more than once. Ensuring her body's aches never faded but endlessly compounded.

The goddess had truly abandoned her, just as she had her mother. The Seelie Court was her cruel and unforgiving home now, a prison she was trapped in with no future.

Thazin grunted and let out a groan as he finished, his grip loosening, as Nova fell limply. "You should count yourself blessed by me for not handing you off as a toy for the orcs. I hear their whispers of cruel desire; they would have you begging for me," he growled out as he let her drop to the floor.

Nova heaved for breath as tears rushed down her cheeks, terrified to move. After a few moments, Thazin dropped to his knees and wrapped a hand around her throat, the other grabbing her braid so forcefully, her eyes peeled open to stare up at him. "If I ever hear of you disobeying another servant again, I'll have them flogged. Do you understand?" he said as he shook her by the hair.

"Yes," Nova wheezed out, her heart pounding in her ears, as she felt his knee come between her legs and she spread them wide. She expected his semi-hard shaft, but what came was the handle of a guard's sword, as he shoved it inside her with one brutal push, forcing her open.

The shredding of her walls and torturous invasion caused Nova to let out a bellow of agony. "You're worthless!" the prince spat out in reply, as he continued to press deeper inside her. Nova whimpered, her tears mixing with the blood on the floor, as

Thazin left the sword handle buried in her.

He bit his palm and dribbled his blood onto her lips; the same ritual that always kept her alive through these tortuous evenings, as he forced his hand over her mouth, smearing his blood on her lips. She could taste the vibrant magic in it, as he gave her just enough to keep her passively obedient with craving, but then he pulled his hand away just as quickly, so as to never allow her to fully feed.

It was a taste that would heal the injuries he'd caused, before leaving her to lick up the rest like a starving mongrel. She would have done anything to have more… to feel a full and sated belly but once.

After she'd lapped up the last of his blood on the floor, he took her by the hair again, dragging her face to his crotch and forcing himself inside her mouth, rutting her throat roughly. "Clean it. Do your job."

She could taste herself on him and the remnants of the magic that healed her. If he had been kinder, she would have happily given herself to him, yet he only ever craved to leave her in misery, even when she made her best efforts.

Nova could feel him twitch against her tongue, and he let out a groan as he spilled himself into her throat, before throwing her into the corner where her bed was propped.

"Your room is putrid. Remove this stench by morning," he hissed, gathering his robes around him and taking ahold of his sword. "It will surely excite the chieftain of the guard if you don't," he added before leaving with a slam of the door

Nova took the rag she'd managed to get from another servant

and tried to clean the mess. All the while her tears ran, diluting the mixed bodily fluids on the floor even more, as she cried softly, wondering why she could not just die.

She had given up seeing any life beyond the misery. Dreams had become the taunting nightmares of a wasted spirit.

After finishing cleaning, Nova curled up on her mattress, shivering despite the summer heat, and she closed her eyes, wishing for the sweetest oblivion of sleep; the closest she ever truly came to a reprieve from his majesty.

CHAPTER 2

THE SLAVE AND THE GIANT

Nova's copper eyes stared back at her in the reflection of the small, scratched and smudged mirror in her quarters, while she attempted to buff the imperfections with a rag and spit. Her quarters were chokingly confined, with rough stone walls and a cold, hard floor; the thin straw mattress in the corner her only furniture, and the lone barred window letting in only the faintest streams of sunlight. Signs of her enslavement were everywhere, with copper shackles covered in a dark patina hanging from the walls, and her meager belongings being kept in a small wooden trunk, etched with the prince's seal. Her vibrant, dark blue hair was pulled into a braid that ran from her scalp to the middle of her back, and a variety of tattoos adorned her flesh, most of which symbolized that she was mere property. Her body was sore from the cruelty the prince had unleashed upon her the night before.

From her earliest memory, she had served the Seelie Crown Family. In her youth, she had fought back with a spur of rebellion, but now, after centuries had gone by, she simply accepted it.

The morning grows late. Perhaps his majesty has drunken himself stupid? she thought with an errant glimmer of hope that she would have a day or two free from him. He never could handle his spirits well.

Suddenly, there was an abrupt bang against her door before the prince's gruff orders bellowed through the wood, startling her breathless. "Ready yourself! The King has summoned us to his private chambers." His voice, despite its enchanting elegance, left her feeling as if ichor ran down her back.

I would take the Feywilds over another day of his torment, she silently pleaded to the gods in her mind.

When she opened the door, the prince stood there, tall and handsome, sharp features prominent, before stomping off to his room, his golden hair elegantly flowing behind him. He wore robes of the finest silks accented with jewels and gold filigree, the crystal dagger glinting at his hip. To any passerby, he appeared every bit the regal fae noble he seemed to be, but when Nova met his eyes, their beauty was only superficial. Behind the striking emerald color was a deep, piercing malice. It was the look of a cat toying with its prey before taking the killing bite.

The prince's charm and fair appearance hid the blackness of his soul, which had caused Nova to suffer for centuries. She knew all too well the cruelty he could inflict with merely a word or a flick of his wrist.

Nova stepped out of her room and stood with her arms behind her back, her head lowered, and she waited patiently in this position for near ten minutes until the prince came out of his room wearing his most regal robes and jewelry. As he walked past her without a word, he snatched her by the braid and dragged her along with him, her tears already rushing to her eyes. She attempted to keep up with him but the way he pulled at her made it difficult, even causing her to trip and fall into the stone wall on a few occasions. These were the moments that made her wish the prince's wrath would finally end her, as even when she put in her best efforts and did exactly as she was told, there was only ever a harsh hand.

"Nova, get up!" the prince shouted at her, dark orange magic glowing at his fingertips as she slowly pushed herself off the wall. Alas, she wasn't quick enough to her feet for his taste, so the prince summoned his magic to course through the slave markings on her body, and she suddenly felt as if dozens of daggers were slicing across her flesh. She cried out pushing herself to her feet as fast as she could in desperate need of relief from the prince's magical onslaught. Her eyes were locked on him, this cruel man with a shoulder-length golden mane, lithe yet standing near two heads above her.

As he released his magical hold on her, his hand crushed her throat and shoved her against the wall, knocking the wind from her lungs as his other forearm slammed against her chest. She was used to having his hand at her throat to the point she no longer panicked from it, so she only had to deal with the daze she felt having her head crash against the wall. "My prince! I am terribly sorry!" she wheezed out, knowing if she didn't apologize, he would only become crueler.

"Don't be sorry, just be better." The prince's tone came out like vile venom, as the searing pain of his magic burned from his palm into her neck. Once he'd pulled his hand away, the pain began to migrate and grow in intensity, and she muffled herself, knowing that if she cried, he'd only make it worse and worse until she fainted from the shock.

If only the gods had taken me alongside Mama… came the same thought that would run through her mind in these moments and leave her feeling empty.

Far down the halls, she caught the gaze of an amber eyed giant with his companion, and the giant's imposing size immediately struck her. He stood three heads above the prince, with a burly frame, and his arms were bare, covered in a pelt of black and white hair, and scars etched into his skin that spoke of many battles. An unruly mane of salt and pepper hair fell to his waist, matching his great swirling beard, with strange glyphs and tattoos marking his body. At his hip hung a massive broadsword, nearly as long as she was tall, and his face was stern, with a strong boxy jaw. But it was in his eyes that she found the heat of a lit hearth that ran across her skin, the type of eyes that made her imagine dashing toward him and huddling in his embrace for safety. When he raised his oversized fist to his chest, something about the gesture gave her fleeting hope, before he stepped into the King's Chambers, having to duck to clear the doorway.

The halls of the palace were cavernous, with vaulted ceilings that arched high overhead, and intricate stained-glass windows casting colorful shadows across the polished marble floors. Tapestries and paintings depicting fae legends lined the walls, interspersed with ornate sconces holding enchanted flames. As they walked, Nova could hear the echoing footsteps of the prince and her own, mixed with the murmurs of other servants going about their tasks. The air was thick with perfumes and floral scents from the extravagant arrangements decorating each hallway. It was a lavish yet cold and lifeless splendor.

Nova stepped into the King's chambers, bowing deeply before the most powerful fae in the Seelie Court. The Council Chambers were immense, with a towering domed ceiling painted with intricate murals of fae history. Ornate chandeliers holding hundreds of flickering candles illuminated the room with ethereal green and blue hues. Polished white marble was spread across the floors, with purple veins running through it like spider webs. At the far end sat the King's gilded throne, encrusted with jewels and plush velvet cushions. Banners with the Royal crest hung on the walls, along with masterfully painted portraits of previous kings. And yet, despite all of this finery, just as with the rest of the palace, it all felt empty.

She stood beside the amber eyed giant and his companion, who she hadn't even properly noticed before, and although the giant stood three and a half heads above his fae companion, it was he who left her fearful for her own life more than the prince ever had.

His amethyst-colored eyes carried an all seeing sharpness, that looked as if they valued no life and exacted cruelty beyond imagination on an impulse, and short yet finely cared for inky black hair and a well-groomed matching beard that was shortly trimmed to his cheeks. He wore robes that elegantly outshone even the King's and the prince's; a grave offense in most cases, and yet this fae was, by just the sense of his aura, far beyond the King and prince in terms of power – wielding the sort of might that was only found in the hands of a god. She knew who he was; she heard whispers around the Court, telling a tale of the only fae to be exiled from the Ether, only to return on a whim; stronger even than the Justicar, a group of powerful fae women who arbitrated the disputes between the Courts and hunted the worst criminals in the land.

"Father! This male dresses in such a disrespectful way! I care no—" the prince shouted out as he stood beside Nova, only to be cut off by the villainous fae. "Prince Thazin, despite your inflated ego and meaningless title, I have no desire to hear a word from your lips. Silence yourself before I am required to put your father in the position of needing a new heir. I would depose you the moment his crown rested upon your oily hair," the villainous fae elegantly stated, dismissing the prince.

"Son, do as you are told. The male before you is no simple fae. He has felled those far more powerful than you with little effort and less reason. I do not wish for blood to be spilled in my chambers," the King scolded, before leaning back into his throne with a dismissive sigh as he focused his gaze back on the amethyst eyed male. "To what do we owe this violation of your exile, Ajax?" the King said, with clear disdain for the fae before him.

Why am I here? A male like this surely would have no interest in the prince's plaything? Nova pondered to herself as she tried her darndest to remain focused. Court dealings always left her feeling dreadfully bored.

"Exile is not within my understanding. No realm is out of reach for me, as you're aware. I have come to you because a rather undesirable rodent hides in your court. I will only make you this offer once, either you hand him over, or I will besiege your Court with a wrath that has left gods cowering," Ajax stated pointedly, a threat that had Nova fearful that the King would incur the aforementioned destruction. The giant beside Ajax leaned down to whisper something in Ajax's ear, before standing up straight. "Ah, as well as your son's slave, Valen here would like her freed and placed into our care."

The King's face contorted in vile frustration, and he opened his mouth to speak, but Thazin burst out first, "Nova'ivar is my slave! She is bound to me!" Spit spewed from the prince's mouth as he spoke, and he reached for his sword, just as a being of pure shadow, with a mass of silvery hair that flowed unbound by the laws of nature, projected out from Ajax's core to grab his throat and force him down to his knees, pressing him roughly into the raw onyx stone floors that surrounded the throne.

A dissonant whisper that carried only the promise of death suddenly came from all directions in the room. "You are insignificant!" The prince's face twisted in agony, as the shadow invaded his mind, and causing his eyes to flood with purple and black magic, as he fell back limp against the ground.

A foreign soft and cooling touch of magic flooded her entire body, as all but one of the inked marks faded from her flesh, leaving only the elegant mark at the center of her chest that was the fae character for Three New Moons, the state of the moons on the day of her birth that determined her full name. Every bit of magic that bound her to the prince was lifted in that moment, and she felt a sense of relief that was near overwhelming. Her copper eyes flooded with tears, which she tried to blink away, only to find a tsunami of whimpers escaping her. Without a thought, she buried herself into the side of the giant, just as she'd wished to do earlier.

"Ajax, banish your shadow, please. My son will cease his behavior and I will aid you. Have your companion take Nova'ivar to the Northern Gardens. I know she is fond of them. When she is calm, she may gather her things. In the meantime, you and I will discuss the rodent you wish to exterminate." The King spoke seemingly in no rush, his tone careless to his own son's torture, offering only a grimace at the entire debacle. "She is Sela'mann's daughter. Are you sure you wish to take that upon your hands?" he asked.

"I am certain this lost little moon child holds a calling beyond your halls," Ajax said as he stepped between the giant,

Nova, and the King, and Nova found an odd sense of safety in him in that moment.

She paid little attention to anything after the giant named Valen scooped her into his arms, his hold on her a warmth she'd always craved, and for the first time in her life she experienced it in that moment. Once they were out of the King's Chambers, she bawled unabashedly into his massive chest. She'd never even imagined she'd find herself in the position of being freed from the prince's cruelty, let alone his magic, no longer having to dread the feeling of her own flesh. She cried more and more, as if she had unleashed eons of her misery upon this giant, soaking his tunic.

Valen carried her to the Northern Gardens, and as they entered through the ivory archway embroidered with images of the three moons, Nova's senses came alive. The gardens were riotous with color, with emerald leaves on the canopy of trees overhead, bushes with vibrant pink and purple flowers, heavy with perfume, at eye level, and marble pathways lined with moss and lush grass weaving through the greenery. She could hear the gentle burble of numerous fountains and streams that threaded throughout the landscape as they walked, and at the center there stood a majestic willow tree, its long leafy tendrils swaying in the breeze, their colors an untamed barrage. The fresh floral scents mingled with the earthy smell of soil, as Valen settled on a purple and green marble bench under the willow, its curved shape perfectly contouring Nova's body as she wept, soaking his tunic, while the peaceful surroundings gradually eased her spirit.

After what felt like an eternity of wailing, Nova inhaled slowly, finding herself able to breathe finally, as she silently laid against the giant for several more minutes before a whimpering tone left her lips. "Your name is Valen, right...?" She gave a sniffle and reached to rub her eyes, only to be surprised by the kerchief she found in his large, outstretched hand. She gingerly took it and wiped her tears away.

"Yes. Name Valen." A gruff, deeper than thunder voice erupted from him, with a tone softer than silk. The smile beneath the overgrowth of hair around his mouth was enough to bring her to giggle softly.

"Why did you free me?" she inquired, worried that he was planning to enslave her again. She felt her stomach sink into a bottomless pit at the thought.

"Slavery unacceptable. Spend eons caged, Ajax freed long ago. Now free Nova," Valen replied as a small black kitten unearthed its little head from his robes and let out its best meow.

Nova couldn't help but giggle at the indignant mew of the kitten, and she patted its head gently. "What do I do now? I don't know what a free life is like..."

"Live as please. Find happiness, love, friends, self. Freedom journey never ends. Always more!" Valen said, so cheerfully that she found herself excited at the idea of being able to truly take on a life that she'd spent so long dreaming of, yet she feared she would fail and lose it all.

"I... I don't know how to do any of that... Where do I go?" Nova's next question came quickly; she was anxious about the concept of freedom, an idea she'd heard of but never thought would be hers to live.

"With us," he replied with a resolute nod. He was so softly spoken, yet he inspired her.

"I can come with you? Yes! I don't want to be here! I never wish to see the Seelie Court again!" she cheered out. Despite her anxiety, she was excited about whatever life would offer her, if it meant the gentle giant would be there with her.

"Get stuff now?" Valen asked as he set her to her feet and she gave him a nod.

"I'll get it myself… I want to walk alone to my room. Can I meet you and Ajax at the palace entrance?" When Valen had given her a nod, she did her best to wrap her arms around him before taking off to her quarters.

⟡

Nova moved through the palace halls in silence to her room, stopping at her door as she realized that this would be her last time coming and going from here. A swell of emotion hit her as she said goodbye to the only home she'd ever known, although it was laced with pain as she recalled sitting in her mother's lap as she brushed her hair while regaling her with tales of faraway lands. She wouldn't miss these walls, but the memories would linger.

She stepped in front of the mirror and pulled it from the wall, setting her mother's copper ring on her left ring finger. The smooth metal warmed against her skin, the engraved pattern of vines and leaves a familiar texture under her thumb as she spun it. Then, she tucked the silver-plated brush into a pocket of her outfit, its bristles worn but still soft, strands of her own blue hair tangled within.

She flashed her brightest smile, revealing a vampire's fangs. The prince punished her anytime he saw them, claiming they were brutish and ugly, but she'd always liked the small twin points herself. "Freedom…" she whispered to herself in the mirror, a word she'd never dared think of as it brought her sadness. Now though, it became the greatest joy of her life.

The gods have answered your prayers for freedom, Mama, she thought, as her cheeks ached from smiling, the corners of her eyes misting with tears.

She raised a hand to touch the single remaining tattoo on her chest and she shut her eyes, taking a few moments to meditate one last time in her quarters. However, her meditation was short-lived as her door burst off its hinges, and there stood the prince, his neck scarred with black, horrifying marks. His bloodshot emerald eyes were brimming with fury, as his hand went for her braid and he threw her against the wall, holding her there as he reached for her pants and tore them away. Next came his hand, spearing between her legs, nails clawing into her.

"You didn't think I'd let you leave the palace, did you?! You'll die before you ever taste freedom!" His other hand moved to crush her throat, squeezing the life from her as she could feel him freeing himself from his robes and spearing into her with his shaft. His thrust was the harshest he'd ever given to her as her hips and back got cut up against the wall. When he finally freed his hand from her throat to punch her in the face twice, she let out a howl of pain, hoping her saviors would hear her.

Why couldn't he have done this on any other day but today? she silently sobbed to herself, her mouth gooey and clammy as she sucked in as much air as she could.

Just then, a monstrous roar came out of nowhere, and her quarters were wreathed in brilliantly colorful flames of varying shades of the entire spectrum. One moment the prince's weight was crushing her against the wall, and the next he was in the air, with Valen's large palm locked around his slender throat. The prince bucked and kicked to free himself, only to be bellowing in agony as his entire body erupted in the same vibrant flames. In moments, he was little more than a pile of ash on the floor, with only his dagger remaining. Valen then removed one of his massive furs and wrapped it around Nova. Beneath them he was wearing a tunic and leather pants, as he carried her out from her room, heading to the exit.

Thazin is dead... am I truly free of him at last? The thought rang through her mind. Despite having witnessed it, she couldn't comprehend such a turn of Fate.

Soon, they met with Ajax at the palace entrance, and he noticed how Valen was carrying Nova. "Did you end him?" Ajax asked, as he snapped his fingers and the fabric of the world seemed to rip open, revealing a gateway, swirling with perceivably limitless magic. As he moved his hand, the sleeve of his robe glided back, revealing the shimmering fabric underneath.

It appeared to be made of silk in a deep purple hue that shifted to blue and black, as if the colors were dancing gracefully. The ornate runic designs along the cuffs and collar glinted, just like the light of his gateway to a fate beyond the Seelie Court.

"Yes," Valen replied as he ran his hand over Nova's back gently.

"Good. He didn't deserve to draw breath. Shall we go? We have things to handle elsewhere. Well, I do. You and Nova should rest," Ajax said as he took the first step into the portal.

What kind of life awaits me beyond? Nova wondered, as Valen stepped inside and the vortex consumed them.

CHAPTER 3

FREEDOM'S FIRST EVENING

The brief seconds traversing the rift were the most vibrant and colorful moments of Nova's life, as, an instant later, the array was replaced by an elegant foyer, with marble statues flanking an entrance adorned by an Ethereal oak door. Nova could tell by the hues of green, blue, purple, and pink in the wood's grain. *What lay beyond the door?* She felt intimidated by the magnitude of the home surrounding her, along with the entrance that would lead to the rest of her life.

When the momentary dazzle of her speedy arrival had worn off, she realized she was in a disheveled state, and she found herself ready to ask for a bath, as Valen carried her somewhere, leaving Ajax's company for an unknown location. As they walked away, Ajax spoke. "Freshen yourself up. You shall enjoy a warm meal once you're comfortable. I will get you a wardrobe until you've found your own tastes. Enjoy your bath." She gave

Ajax a nod and soon found herself in a bathroom lined with black marble, with a tub so large that three Valens could fit in it.

Valen settled her on the counter as he ran the bath. "I've only had cold baths…" she mumbled to herself, wondering how the tub before her worked. She had always been the one carrying the water for the prince's baths and stoking the flames for heat. She pulled her braids loose to unleash the mass of dark blue curls and waves, getting lost in her thoughts as her fingers ran along the oily strands.

"Make warm. Promise. No more cold baths," Valen said, offering her a gentle smile. The male before her was something she'd never encountered – compassionate for the sake of another.

She watched as the water that filled the tub shimmered like diamonds, as steam rose in an enticing, visible dance of wisps, and a sense of warmth flared up in her belly alongside an inexplicable flutter. "Can I have a hot bath?" she asked, her voice trembling in anticipation.

"Yes. Soothe body." Valen said, turning to face her before sitting on the edge of the tub.

She sucked back the tears that stung her eyes, feeling terrible that all he'd ever seen her do was erupt. With a deep sniffle, Nova met his gaze. "Thank you…" she whispered, looking into his amber eyes that matched her own. Their closeness allowed her to take in his scent of baked sweets and hearth fires.

"Take bath now?" Valen asked, wiping away the tears sitting in the corners of her eyes. When she nodded, he stepped out of the bathroom. "Wait outside. Take time. Supper after," he said, giving her that warm smile which eased her. All the passing years of misery, and yet she was so blown away by how he aided her in finding comfort.

Alone in the bathroom, she stripped the furs bearing Valen's scent off and looked at her body in the mirror, the markings she had born for most of her life now gone. Even her scars faded to dull, noticeable imperfections across her otherwise pale skin. The only magic within her now was her own. She moved to the tub and settled into the waters, so blissfully hot she wished she could stay there for eternity, as she submerged herself and curled up; the heat soothing her aching body and soul. Pains that, despite being healed, remained from Thazin's endless cruelty.

She spent well over an hour in the bath, half of the time lying still in the floral scented waters, and the other half scrubbing herself raw with all the different soaps, until she discovered a slick bar that left her thinking of kitchens and baked goods, so savory yet sweet as it was.

She emerged from the bathroom wrapped in plush towels, feeling clean for the first time in her life, the scented bar in hand. "Hey Valen… what is this scent?" He was a quiet male and nothing felt worse than disrupting his peace as she kept her voice lower than a mouse's.

Valen sat on the floor playing with his kitten, and he got to his feet and plopped it on his shoulder, "Vanilla. Bath good?" Nova turned toward the bathroom and placed the bar back in the bath before returning to Valen.

She gave him a nod as she made a mental note of the vanilla, her pale skin reddening as she sank her front teeth into her lower lip. "It was amazing… you are a kind master!" she let out with a beaming smile, only to find her heart sinking at the brief look of dismay on Valen's face.

When his amber gaze flicked toward her, he shook his head, dismissing her. "Not master. Nova free. Remember?" The massive male shifted from standing up to resting on his knees so he could be near eye level with her. "Promise." He gave her his gruff and charming smile through the thick brush.

What am I supposed to be if not a slave? the voice in her mind said; a voice that could only see a path into her past.

She gave Valen a nod and smiled back as his hand came to her cheek, and she shut her eyes for a moment, basking in his intense warmth. His kind way of reminding her of her freedom made her feel blessed by the gods to have aligned her fate with his, as she opened her eyes, only to find herself shocked as she noticed the harsh scar that crossed between his eyebrows to the right corner of his jaw, even leaving a mark over his right eye. It made her heart sink for a moment to imagine someone would hurt him in such a way, and she spun her mother's ring with her thumb; the sensation soothing her. "Thank you, Valen. Can you show me where my clothes are?"

Valen gestured for her to step back, as he shifted and took on his usual titanic stature, and she stared at his belly before craning her head up to look at him. "I have seen no one as tall as you! How did you get so big, Valen?" she inquired, cocking her head to the side.

He gave a shrug. "Parents maybe taller? Never knew." He spoke in a near whisper as he led her toward another room.

She frowned, wishing she could have shared her mother with him, as she fell silent in contemplation, no response seeming adequate. In the end, she decided to give his hand a tight squeeze.

"Dinner. Three-day Atlantean fish stew. Ready?" Valen said with a sense of giddiness hidden beneath his calm tone, as he opened the door for Nova before she could ponder the stew. The elegance of her room shocked her. "I live like a princess!" she shouted out, eyeing the plush bed with its dark cobalt blanket atop undyed linens that looked heavenly, with a white cloudlike pillow. She even had a simple vanity, yet to her this was a thing of regality.

Is that the bed I get to sleep in? she wondered to herself, eyes running over what looked like the most luxurious place she'd ever set eyes on.

"Not very fancy. Good and comfy," Valen said as he patted her back and grinned down at her.

Nova stepped toward the vanity and dropped her towel, beginning to look in the storage and the closet. She heard Valen turn to walk away. "You won't tell me what to wear? Watch me dress?"

"No. Privacy important. You pick," Valen declared as he crossed the door's threshold. Nova's brow, lips, and nose contorted in confusion, but she let him keep going.

He is a peculiar male, she mused to herself.

After blowing air between pursed lips and causing them to clap together, her eyes drifted to the mirror, tracing her finger over the singular remaining tattoo. Freedom was such a foreign concept to her, and she felt awful for messing it up. Determined to do better, she pulled her brush out and began running it through her hair.

Nova stepped out from the door of her new room and looked up and down the hall, wearing a pair of comfortable yet conforming wool trousers and a dark red tunic that was baggy on her. Her dark blue hair was freed in a thick wavy mass, and her feet were hugged by a pair of heavenly soft slippers. She spun her ring thrice before moving ahead, feeling a whole slew of emotions, but mostly, for the first time, she felt alive.

Taking off toward Valen's door, she noticed it was ajar, and she gave it a light knock as she found herself greeted by him walking into her line of sight with only a towel around his hips. A thick brush of black curly hairs with faint splashes of white ran across Valen's torso, and he sported a physique akin to what she imagined the heroes of her mother's spoken tales did. His scars even matched those of the mythic males she'd loved as a child. "I'm sorry! I'll wait for you!" she yelled out, before turning with her back against the wall, holding her breath, as a wave of fear crashed over her. With her eyes shut, the image of one scar came to mind – right where his heart was, there was a grave and deep mark. She tried to imagine what would bring someone to stab him in the chest.

Her only respite came when she spun her ring without even

thinking about it and a sense of calm was restored. After that, she walked up and down the hall, fidgeting, worried he'd punish her for disturbing his bathing rituals. Lost in racing thoughts of uncertainty, she yelped in terror when Valen seemed to appear right behind her and his hand came to her shoulder as he smiled. "No worry. Eat supper now?" Such a tender tone was mind-boggling coming from the male before her, who she was certain inspired fear in most because of his hardened appearance.

Her pounding heart slowed to a steady beat and she nodded. "Yes! Please?" she begged him, hoping this meant she wasn't in any trouble. He gestured in the direction they'd be walking, taking slower, shorter strides so she could keep up with him.

"Look nice. Hair beautiful. Nova vampire? Need blood? Can have mine."

Her face lit up with a bloom of searing heat at his words, as she took a moment to contemplate how to respond, embarrassment running through her mind. She always needed blood, but she only ever got it from an animal once every few months. "Yes… I have had none in many months. You sure? I feel bad biting you. Thank you for complimenting my hair. I've always loved it," she replied in rapid succession, as she ran a hand through her thick blue waves, a tremble racking her body.

He shook his head and opened up the door to the dining room. A dark-red, oak table, large enough to seat seven people, took up the majority of the space, the chairs so elegant in their lush design, she imagined Ajax had created them himself. Goblets, bowls, and cutlery of copper lined the table, and while it was not lined with a beauty to mask empty hearts, there was a simple elegance to the dining room; a room that she could imagine enjoying her meals in every day.

"No feel bad. Don't mind. Nova needs blood. Have lots. Promise!" Valen's wide smile came to reassure her, and she tucked herself against his side in an immediate response. It felt so natural to lean into his warmth, as she noticed a low rumble in his chest, nothing like a growl or anything so sinister, but more like a sated, content sound; one that left her thinking of when she'd see the animals brought from Terra to the zoo in the Seelie Court.

"Thank you… can I have it before we eat?" She pulled back from his strong core, staring upward, searching for something to read on his face; any sign that stopping now would be the best call.

He gave her a nod and pulled out a chair and sat down. "Wrist? Neck?" he wondered aloud, tugging at his collar.

"Neck? I don't know… I've never fed off of a person. Only animals before they were to be turned into meals…" She looked down, embarrassed by her admission.

"Neck fine. Sit in lap." he invited her, a proposal she was joyous to take him up on, as she pushed herself up to his neck, nudging his dense beard aside only to find yet more scars. Her mother had similar ones – those of forced feedings. Dread filled her once more at the thought of forcing him to endure being bitten when his neck bore such cruel marks.

This is wrong…. I can't… her mind raced.

"Are… you sure?" she asked again, needing his permission to go forward. Feeling her breath hitch in her chest.

"Yes. Scars ancient. Take all Nova need," he uttered in a sincere yet playful tone, as his hand came to her back and offered her a slow rub that settled her frayed nerves.

She leaned forward and drew his scent in. It was a warm, delightful musk, with a hint of sweetness to it that tickled her nose in the best way. "I'm sorry. I hate that I have these needs," she whispered against his throat, only to be shushed by him.

"Don't apologize. All have needs. Want Nova's met," he said softly, yet firmly enough to give her confidence that her barbaric needs were okay in this moment.

She sank her fangs as gently as she could into his vein, and his blood tasted way better than any animal she'd had. It was subtle and complex in flavor, and after several pulls, she felt sated, but she still took a couple more gulps before removing her lips and lapping at the marks with her tongue to seal them. She longed to identify the various flavors of his blood, but her limited exposure to only gruel and scraps hindered her palate's refinement.

As she leaned back against him, Valen greeted her with a kerchief, dabbing the blood from her lips. "Feel better?" His question came with cheer countered with worry in his eyes.

She flattened her lips together and tried to read his face, unable to see anything other than a warm soul, as she wished to know what had left him so worried. "Much. Your blood is delicious…best I've ever had!" She let her feeling of contentment take over her as she molded herself to the male, basking in his endless heat once more. She loved the look of pride on his face, so happy to have been able to just help her in any way he could. Never in her life had she imagined such a person to exist, never mind that she could deserve his sweet nature.

After several long, and silent yet comforting moments in his embrace, she stood up and took his hand, pulling him to the scent of what she knew was the stew he'd made. "You must be hungry… let's eat!" she cheered out.

He was already up and gesturing for her to take a seat next to him. "I get. Nova relax," he said with a firmness to his tone that left her only to comply without even a thought of resistance.

She gave a sharp exhale to banish her confusion before settling in her seat and having her chair gently pushed in by Valen. It took a few seconds for a bowl, made of the same material as her ring, filled with the most delicious smelling stew, to be placed before her, and for Valen to be sitting across from her. His bowl looked akin to a small cauldron and his spoon a ladle. Once he started eating, she followed suit with squeals of joy erupting from her as the flavors of the stew were a rapturous journey; the chunks of meat so tender they fell apart at the touch of the spoon, as the spices lit small yet pleasant flames across her forked tongue.

One silent meal later, she was leaning back in her seat, looking at her empty bowl. Her belly filled with stew, and her craving for blood fully satisfied, she suddenly felt exhausted, as she let out a long yawn and watched Valen rise from his seat to clean up. She wanted to help but felt immobile in her fullness. Her belly felt different from the typical hunger pangs she was used to. She felt a faint sense of being bloated, yet a comforting wave of fulfilled warmth swept across her. By the time Valen had finished cleaning, she was already asleep. She failed to process him lifting her up against his chest and burying her into his warmth at first, as he left the now clean dining room, heading for the hall where their rooms were. Her only instinct was to curl up as much as she could against him and let the comfort take her away, as his beard tickled the back of her neck, drawing faint giggles from her. Without a thought, she speared her fingers into the rough mass of hair, thrilled by its coarse texture.

The last thing she recalled before slipping away into slumber was being tucked into the silky sheets and blanket of the bed in her room.

CHAPTER 4

SOARING

When she awoke, the scent of fatty meats and eggs being cooked caught her nose, and she snapped upright from her most peaceful slumber, a very welcome deviation from the sleepless nights she was used to.

Her mind drifted off imagining Valen in the kitchen preparing breakfast, so she pushed herself from her bedding and stripped off her clothes, only to change into the fluffiest pair of pants she'd ever touched, and a sheer low-cut tunic that exposed her chest as she was feeling overheated. Nova crammed her feet into the pair of slippers and took off while brushing her hair, following the scents that had her stomach gnawing away at her very existence. She burst into the kitchen, bubbling with excitement for her first true day of freedom, yearning to see what was out there in the world beyond the Court she'd spent her whole life in – all of the wondrous places her mother had spun tales of.

There stood Valen, handling quite an extensive selection of meats and fishes that she'd never seen before, as well as what she knew were sausages. The Seelie King had always eaten his breakfast with sausages. She stepped behind Valen and looked at the food he was cooking. "This food smells real good! It woke me up," she said, turning her head toward him and flashing him a lopsided, fang revealing grin, her eyes searching for his, only to feel her soul being soothed again by his soft gaze.

"Good morning. Sleep well?" His question came out in an even huskier than normal tone, and the deep circles beneath his weary eyes had her wondering if he ever actually slept. She gave him a hug. "Yes, I've never slept better. The bed is so comfy! Thank you for saving me, Valen…" His free arm came around to cage her against his body in a firm embrace. "Do you and Ajax have plans today?" she asked as she huddled against him. The gruff male shook his head. "Then what'll we do?" Her next question came with furrowed brows.

Valen looked away in deep thought. "Show Atlantis. Beautiful city. Have money. Buy Nova things," he said, turning back to her as he flipped the meats he cooked.

"My mother once told me tales of Atlantis! I get to see it?" she shouted as she imagined exploring the endless streets of such a city of wonder. She couldn't help but ask herself how and why fate had turned her life around so.

He gave a nod and handed her a plate of fish, meat, and

sausages before walking with her to the small dining room. Just like the previous night, he pulled her chair out for her and tucked her under the table before taking his place. They ate with a feathered touch, as between bites, Nova chattered away about the tales of Atlantis her mother regaled her with. Once they both finished, Valen cleaned up and continued listening to her rambling in circles.

With the kitchen and dining room tidied, they walked back to her room and Valen gestured to the door. "Dress for outside. Wait here," he said before turning into his own dwelling.

She gave him a nod with a faint pout of puckered lips before heading into her room, only to emerge wearing a beige tunic that looked almost long enough to be Valen's, but she had it cinched at the waist, making it into a short dress that flowed down to her mid-thigh, with a firm pair of hide pants hugging her legs.

It was then that she felt his eyes roam her body for the first time, not to see a freed slave he was helping, but rather taking in someone desirable.

She covered herself, shying away from the way he looked at her, and he turned his head swiftly to avert his gaze. When he did this, she teased her lip with a fang, giving it a gentle bite without breaking the skin. "Do I look good?" she asked, hoping for his approval as her eyes drifted to the floor.

When his war-stained rough hands came up to cup her cheeks, warming her with his touch, she couldn't resist but to lean in. He was like a fire, except no matter how close she got, there was never a burn left behind. His words fell upon her ears, leaving her frozen in place, yet blazing her with joy. "Excited. Lovely."

Satisfied with his reply, she took his hand and attempted to bolt out the door, trying to drag him with her, only to find that Valen wouldn't budge. "Wait," he said, and she stopped in her tracks and watched him.

Her eyes were suddenly drawn to a pair of wings made up of blue, yellow, orange, red, and purple feathers, wreathed in vibrantly colored flames that bloomed out from his back. Nova reached out to touch one of them, and the flames didn't burn, but rather felt just like his usual warmth, the feathers softer than even the finest silks of the Seelie Court. "What are you?" she asked in a low whisper full of wonder.

Valen gave her a sheepish grin, scratching at his bushy beard before he stated, "Phoenix. Can take flying?" She was trying to imagine a phoenix, an enormous bird ablaze with fantastical colors, until his offer caught her ear.

Did you ever know this male Valen, Mama? He is so different; kind, yet powerful, she thought. She liked to think her mother would have adored Valen as much as she did.

"Like the Dragons? Yes, I would love to fly! Please Valen, can we go now?" He gave her a grin and a nod as she begged and pleaded.

"Yes, we go. Turn around," he said, causing her to spin around without question, trying not to lose her last remnants of control in excitement at the idea of soaring through the sky.

I'm getting to take to the skies, Mama. I wish you could join us, she thought as she bounced on the balls of her feet excitedly, squealing out in shock as Valen scooped her up and carried her off.

⁎⸱⸱ ❦ ⸱⸱⁎

She was hoping to see lovely stonework, but at first all that filled her view bore the beauty that nature provided in the form of a dense jungle bearing such vibrant greenery and a cacophony of beasts erupting in the distance. She turned her head back in confusion, only for Valen to point ahead, and as she followed the direction of his large finger, her eyes caught sight of something more beautiful than she could have ever imagined. The city that was stretched out before her was far more stunning and glorious than the Seelie Court Palace itself.

The city was vast, with a glittering dome of magic arching gracefully over the lavish buildings below it. Channels of water flowed almost effortlessly and unimpeded alongside the streets and avenues, and at its center, a large temple stood in its impressive glory. The buildings were a collection of beautiful arched door frames, wide windows, and polished stone structures, with even the simplest of homes looking like a work of art in its own standing.

It was inhabited mostly by fae, elves, and humans, who were just as beautiful as the buildings themselves, the skin tones of the people in the distance ranging from pale to dark, and not just the pinkish hue of skin she was used to, but blues, greens, and even purples in the case of some elves.

The proud city bore the flowing and graceful design of its

builders: the back swept tipped ear elves. With nature themed stained glass on each window, the city bustled with trade and life, a cascading array of concentric circles alternating between land and bodies of water. There were four behemoth towers, one at each of the cardinal points, made of a brilliant, perfectly white stone, polished to be lavishly smooth and reflective.

She could hear the bustle of trade going on around and across this mighty city of Atlantis, a place far more beautiful than even her mother's tales could describe, and she wanted to see all of it. "We get to explore this city?" she asked with excitement and trepidation running through her. All she could think of in this moment of overwhelming hope for the future was to spin her ring. Valen gave her a nod and jogged two dozen paces away, only for his body to become consumed in a vibrant display of flames of every imaginable color. When they dissipated, a massive bird that had to be five times his height stood, its feathers the same brilliant plumage that he'd showed earlier. He had dark slate gray and inky black feathers across most of his body, with the tips of his wings bearing untamed hues much like the inferno that had swallowed his prior form.

He pointed his hooked beak to a spot on his back, which she climbed onto, and she held on tight as he took off toward the clouds, soaring through the skies. Wind rushed through her hair and made keeping her eyes open a challenge worth the tears. She could taste the salty spray of the ocean with each breath, the foreign air fresh in her body as she closed her eyes to take in the sensations of flying like a dragon. "If this is all a dream, I never want to wake up!" she shouted at the top of her lungs.

Nova reached her hand out to touch the dome in a moment of impulsive curiosity as they flew just above Atlantis, and her hand passed through it as if breaking the surface of water, only it remained intact. An intense buzzing shot up her left arm, and her teeth were vibrating even after she withdrew her hand. "I wish we could stay in the sky forever!" she bellowed out, not worried if Valen could hear her.

She couldn't help but giggle and cheer as he performed elegant maneuvers in the sky, and the more wildly he flew, the tighter she clung as her squeals of joy grew so loud, she was sure her voice would be hoarse later on.

When they finally descended, Valen shifted into his normal form, as a vibrant and violent burst of flames surrounded them. He cradled Nova in his arms as they touched down, with her blue and his salt and pepper hair a thickly tangled mess.

She spoke, winded by her roars of jubilation. "That was so amazing, Valen! You can do that whenever you wish?" What shocked her more than anything was when he withdrew a hairbrush from his vest and ran it through her matted locks with the most tender of touches, until the mess of blue on her head was an unknotted, well-kept sea of silky tresses. She then watched as he did his own hair before stashing the brush.

"We shop now. Follow. Emporium. Best clothes," he uttered as he led her through the streets. She felt intimidated by the endless population of elves, fae, humans, shifters, magus, and even the odd vampire. The people of Atlantis were as beautiful as the city itself.

After what felt like an hour of walking, Nova's legs grew tired, so Valen lifted her up and carried her the rest of the way until they arrived at a monument of a building. It looked similar to the temples fae erected in honor of the dragons, and yet she could hear coins bouncing off of counters, as a hoard of voices exchanged terms of negotiation for what she imagined was a place where anyone could buy anything their heart desired.

It made the Seelie markets seem puny and insignificant. Her eyes flicked up at Valen and she tugged on his lapel as she pointed to the words above the mighty door that looked near double Valen's size. "What does that say? I can't read…" she admitted with a bashful averting of her gaze.

"Atlas' Emporium," Valen replied, his focus remaining forward.

"Who is Atlas?" she inquired, as they went through a door that swung open of its own free well to grant them entry.

She noticed him running his fingers through his beard in thought before he explained. "Atlantis King. Atlantis named after King." She felt awestruck at the idea that this monolith of a kingdom was named and built because of one male. As they moved through the densely packed areas, Nova's heart thumped erratically, as so many sensations came at her all at once.

The first thing to really capture her attention was a man holding up glass jars filled with a viscous dark red honey. He was shouting out in a rather convincing tone, although she had no idea what he was saying. Going by the way he waved and pointed at the jar though, she thought it must be some kind of cure all, but what fascinated her was that only humans seemed to gather around him.

The more she allowed her eyes to seek anything that might pique her interest, the more absolutely everything did, right down to the children running about peddling cheap trinkets and baubles. She even caught sight of one or two of them with their fingers in someone else's pockets, and countless small vendors bartering and dealing with beautiful and wildly scented goods that were so pungent she had to pinch her nostrils shut from the onslaught to her senses.

If I were King, I would buy something from everyone, she mused, the idea of having unlimited coffers one she rather enjoyed.

Valen carried her into a large boutique, where her eyes scanned various displays enamored with all sorts of things, until she found herself fixated on a set of accessories, hairpins, and matching ear cuffs made of what looked like the same metal as her ring adorned with elegant designs.

A tawny blonde female elf with hair that ran to her shoulders approached them, and Nova noted her pulled back instead of uplifted tipped ears and tribal markings on her face as she came up from the opposite side of the display. She was homely in demeanor; the type of person that one would imagine favored baking breads and sweets as a favorite pastime. Her voice came out with a vibrant welcome, as if inviting an old friend inside for dinner. "Hello, are you enjoying our wares?"

Nova nodded to her and smiled. "Yes, it is all so lovely. This set is the prettiest, though," she said, pointing to one that had caught her eye. "It must have a grand tale?" she asked, bringing her finger to prod against her own chin.

"My, you have fine tastes. It was worn by the first human Queen of Atlantis, Analyn, a girl from the islands in the Far East. She ruled beside King Atlas for two hundred years before she passed in her sleep. She was a most beloved Queen. They are of the finest orichalcum, just like your ring. They have been in the Emporium since her passing. Many have tried them on, but some say the spirit of Analyn has awaited all these years for the right person to come along and bear them. Would you like to try them on?" the elf woman inquired as she pulled them out.

Nova gave a nod, finding herself in love with the tale of this well adored Queen. "May I?" she pleaded with the saleswoman, who bore an elegant glow as she reached to help Nova fix the ear cuffs and hair pins into place, only then for the kind elf to show her a golden mirror where she stared at herself. She watched the cuffs shape themselves to the curves and tips of her ears.

She is kind like Valen. Are there many kind people out there? she pondered as she felt the woman's hands affix the jewelry. The weight and warmth of the metal came to soothe her much like her mother's ring.

"You look glorious… like a goddess!" The elf woman spoke as Nova turned to Valen, who was smiling and studying her. Valen nodded "Agree. Met many goddesses. Some very jealous." That made Nova's heart sing as she hugged him.

"Can I please have them?" Valen gave a nod as he pulled out

a coin purse, when the elf dismissed him with her hand. "They aren't for sale. Whomever fate intended to have them can leave the Emporium with them. King Atlas felt it would be wrong to sell his Queen's jewelry but knew she wanted them to be worn by others. If fate finds you worthy, you can have them." The grin across her face could be heard within each word.

Without a thought, Nova took off running toward the exit. She wanted – needed – to know if the Queen's jewels and her were meant to be. Upon reaching the blinding sun outside the Emporium, she felt relieved that she could carry them out. She cried out in joy as she felt the weight of the ear cuffs and hair pins. Bracing her back against the wall beside the doors, she spent a few moments thanking Queen Analyn's long past spirit for blessing her in silence.

CHAPTER 5

NEW FRIENDS, SETTLED DEBTS

Panic seized Nova as she scanned the bustling Emporium for Valen. She had been so fixated on the Queen's jewelry that she had accidentally lost her gentle, giant companion. With him the building hadn't felt so intimidating and gargantuan, but now the ivory pillars, elegant designs of countless artisans, seas of voices, and the eye-watering mixture of musk's left her wondering. *Have I ruined my new life over something pretty?*

She peered into the Emporium, only to find that she couldn't spot him, so she went back inside and began searching everywhere, only to learn that the building was far larger and more mazelike in design than she ever would have imagined. Doing her best to avoid being knocked down by the untamed flow of foot traffic, she managed to crash into more walls and pillars than people.

As time dragged on, Nova felt increasingly lost and hopeless; alone in an unfamiliar world. She prayed to find Valen or the woman who'd given her the Queen's accessories, but to no avail. After what felt like hours of searching, she just followed the scent of food.

The Emporium's maze of crowded stalls overwhelmed Nova's senses, as strange tongues filled the air alongside music from unknown instruments. Exotic aromas wafted around her – some spicy, others sweet – as she narrowed her eyes at counters piled high with odd fruits, vegetables, and baked goods of every color. People bargained animatedly in their alien languages, as jeers and laughter erupted often. Nova was afraid that the havoc would consume her.

Stalls, booths, and entire sit-down affairs sprawled up and down the halls of the Emporium as she wandered. The smells were enchantingly delightful as she eyed pretty faced human women carrying platters of little pieces of meat with sticks skewered upward from them, handing them out. She looked for every single person to gain a little morsel. When they spoke to her, it was in a language foreign to her, as she'd only ever known the tongue of fae.

One woman cast a pitying gaze upon her before handing her an entire platter of the most heavenly smelling red meats, and she found a hidden corner and curled up within the shadowy spot while tossing morsels into her mouth. She felt comforted briefly while taking her time to eat and enjoy each individual piece to its fullest extent.

She felt terrible knowing Valen was likely still searching for her. The idea crossed her mind to remain in one spot and perhaps he'd find her? That seemed most wise, like something her mother would instruct her to do.

Nova watched the hustle and bustle of the Emporium around her for what felt like at least an hour, only to be approached by a pair of lightly armored males. The first one spoke in a language foreign to her as he approached her, and she wondered if it was the native language of Atlantis. When she couldn't respond, the second male spoke her familiar fae language. "What are you doing here? Move along!"

"Sire, I am waiting for my companion. A very tall male, with a big bushy black and white beard, and long hair much the same! Have you seen him?" she asked while pushing to her feet. Her heart pounded with excitement thinking they might reunite her with Valen.

The two males conversed back and forth in their foreign tongue, before they grabbed each of her arms to drag her out, she squirmed in their grasp, pleaded to be released, and writhed wildly, finally falling from their hold to the ground and scrambling away.

She made it a dozen steps, only to run into something solid, just as the first guard grabbed a fistful of her hair and yanked her back, causing Nova to yelp as he threw her to his partner. That was when her eyes caught what she'd run into: a female who matched Ajax's height, with blonde hair slung into a neat braid over her shoulder, fierce emerald eyes blazing with wrath, as she reacted to the first guard's brutish manhandling by breaking his nose with the heel of her palm in a swift and precise strike. She was wearing a plain worn bloodstained tunic, alongside a mix-matched pelt of various animals over her shoulders and back.

With the first guard now lying flat on his back, the light previously in his eyes entirely faded, the second guard withdrew his sword from its sheath, shouting at the woman in their foreign language again. With a roll of her sharp emerald gaze, she stepped toward the guard and kicked the sword from his grasp, then she lifted him by the collar of his armor and began rocking him, before sending him flying into a wall, putting him in the same state as his fellow guardsman.

The female then snatched Nova's tunic, pulling her to her feet as she spoke fae. "You're new, aren't you? Ugh, how is it that misfits always seem to cross my path? I know the male you're looking for. Well, I'll keep you out of trouble. Stick with me. I've got a drunken bitch to find. The name's Shanti by the way," the tall blonde said pridefully.

"Sh-ahn-teee?" Nova softly sounded out the name of the fearsome female until she had fingers snapping in her face.

"Yes, that's my name sister, don't wear it out. What's yours?" Impatience littered the female's tone and posture as her arms crossed over her chest.

"Nova…" she exhaled nervously. The brash nature of her new companion was alarming but comforting in its own way, offering the sense that nothing could get in their way as Shanti would just topple it with unrestrained brute force.

"Walk and talk. If I don't find that bitch soon enough, she'll be too many bottles deep and useless. We've got work that needs doing." Shanti spoke as she led Nova through the mazelike structure. "What brings a waif like you here? Atlantis ain't a city for the meek."

"Valen was taking me shopping for clothes, but we got separated. He freed me yesterday," Nova replied, thinking through her answer to ensure it wasn't provoking Shanti.

Shanti let out a brief laugh, and she slapped Nova on the back. "That's great for you! Slavery is horse shit. Valen? I know the big fella. You help me with what Alana and I have to do, and I'll make sure you get home nice and safe to Valen. He still palling around with Ajax?" Nova nodded in reply as they came out from the Emporium and Shanti's focus shifted. Nova had seen trackers in the Ether hunt, and it was a similar behavior of alertness.

"Is Alana your missing friend?" she questioned as Shanti began dragging her along, moving a little too fast for her.

"If by missing you mean drowning in a hole in the wall, then yes. Here she is," Shanti uttered as she came to a stop in front of a tavern. "Now you stay out here. Just post up next to the door, and I'll be out in a minute," Shanti stated, pointing exactly where to stand, before stomping her way inside, using the toe of her boot to open the door.

Nova leaned against the facade of the tavern, even if the wood looked so time worn that it may crumble to dust with just a breath. She waited for Shanti's return, only to overhear the commotion inside; a mixture of rowdy cheers and jeers before a distinctly harsh feminine voice cut through the noise. "Alana! Get your drunken ass moving before I break a bottle over your head." Shanti's shouts burst out from the nearby window, as she spoke the same language as the guards from earlier.

"Oi! Fack ye! Am nae leavin' ya hear!" an unfamiliar voice shouted out in a feminine yet deep drawl, in a brogue that left Nova unsure if they were even proper words. Next came the sound of glass smashing, and moments later, Shanti dragged a woman with incredibly dark, nearing black brunette hair. She was certainly a woman who lived with a hammer in her hand judging by her stout curves and enormous arms. "An' ye got a new friend? Ello' lass!" the clearly drunken woman cheered out in a butchered attempt to speak fae.

Is this what the King always meant when he cursed how the Unseelie spoke? But she's no fae… her scent is familiar. Maybe she's a vampire? Nova wondered as her eyes narrowed when she noticed a trickle of blood behind one of the woman's ears. "I'm Nova…" she uttered softly.

"Alana's me name! Yer taggin' along wit' us?" came the female's cheery question. Nova gave a nod and a small smile. She liked this woman. Despite her demeanor as a drunkard, she could tell there was a kindness to her. "Oi! Jus' lemme give ye something, lass. Bet yer havin' a rough time understandin' others." Alana produced a vibrant orange stone with carvings on it and grinned. "Rune fer helpin' ye. It'll activate when ye can't understand something others say."

Nova took the rune gingerly, and she tucked it into her pocket, all the foreign words from the world around her suddenly sounding understandable. "Thank you, Madam Alana."

"Oi nae a lick o' tha' formality, aye? We're friends! Ain't makin' new friends, grand lass?" Alana's bubbly nature set Nova at ease, as she wondered if it was the drink or just her personality.

Why does the stone work for everyone so clearly yet not Miss Alana? she questioned silently. Nova's brow furrowed in confusion at Alana, as she'd clearly understood her despite the words she spoke sounding foreign. "New friends? I've not really had those before."

"Well, you've got us now, and we've got work to do. Keep up Nova, and try to stay behind one of us," Shanti spoke as she led the new trio ahead and Alana fell back to walking beside her.

"So, what brings a lass like ye to Atlantis? Shanti dinnae say much," Alana inquired as she pulled out a bottle and drank from it, exhaling a breathy sigh of relief.

"Oh… I am from the Seelie Court. I was a slave, but Valen and Ajax freed me. I got lost while out with Valen getting clothes." With a snort of amusement, Alana put her arm around Nova's shoulder and cheered out.

"Well, thank fates fer tha' because now ye made friends! Valen and Ajax ya say? Those two're good lads. Nary a fella who dresses better than tha' Ajax." Alana's chipper lack of sobriety was fun to Nova. She seemed like a good *friend* to have.

"What work do we have to do?" Nova asked as her eyes focused on Shanti, who weaved through the crowds with a purpose, anyone in her path rushing out of the way.

"Collectin' a debt. A fella here owes Shanti quite a lot. Ere's to hopin' it goes well! Slainte!" Alana cheered once more before guzzling down a good portion of her bottle.

"What are you drinking?" Nova asked as she eyed the thick, iridescent purple syrup.

Alana pulled her bottle away from her lips and flashed a deviant smirk. "A brew that I've bullied a buncha' witches into concocting fer me. Now tha birds be selling it and nae even given me a royalty or free brew!" she stated indignantly.

It must be delicious considering how much of it she drinks, Nova thought, as the three females effortlessly glided through the crowds of people in Atlantis. "How did you two meet Valen?" she asked.

"Ages ago. A few fools and I saved him. Caused a whole big scene. He's got a brother! Bird brain's one cooky cookie, though," Shanti explained callously as she kept them on track to their next destination. Nova admired the fierce way the lycaness stomped through the streets, with her squared up shoulders as if at any moment she would be ready to fight. *One day I will be fierce like you, Shanti,* Nova swore in her mind. "Is his brother also a phoenix?" she blurted out.

Shanti shook her head as she tucked some stray golden hairs behind her ear. "Nope. Big T is all brain. He knows magic and math like you wouldn't believe. Makes godly things too," she explained, as Nova began trying to imagine who Valen's brother was. *Is he taller? Does he talk like Valen? Are his eyes the same pretty color?* The series of thoughts consumed her for the rest of their walk, yet no real clarity came to mind.

The trio came upon the entrance of a rather large home, with elegant statues littered across it, and each window being adorned with stained-glass murals of heroic battles. Shanti looked back at Nova and flashed an aggressive grin. "Just watch and learn, Nova," she uttered before slamming the side of her fist twice into the door. As soon as a diminutive Elven man opened it up, Shanti had him by the throat. "Where's Kelvem?"

"Madam! The master isn't taking guests. Please unhan—" the guard stammered out, only for Shanti to thrust him into a nearby wall, embedding him into it as she stomped inside. Shanti's violence startled Nova, and she felt it better to follow silently than question her methods.

Shanti and Alana walked through the halls, kicking doors off their hinges, as they shouted out the name of the male they sought, while all Nova could do was stare. She noticed the illustrious tapestries of ancient tales, a few of them familiar to her as her mother had once told her about them. Spread across the floors were various different rugs made from the pelts of noble beasts, and she could imagine Shanti slaying them effortlessly.

"We ought ta' burn tha place down don' ya think Shanti?" Alana threatened, until a male presented himself with his hands up. *He's given up. Surely the destruction is over with now,* Nova thought as she huddled between the two females.

The man stood tall, yet hung his shoulders in defeat. "Stop! Please!" he shouted with fear dancing in his eyes.

Nova narrowed her gaze at the male, noticing something in one of his hands, but before she could make it out, a weight dropped upon her and she felt a male materialize over her and tackle her down. Another one had Alana on the ground kicking and screaming; he was struggling to keep her down from the looks of it. "'ll tear yer wee balls off!" Alana screeched out.

Shanti, for her part, used the face of the male who tried to bring her down to paint the wall red by grinding his nose against it. When she had finally released his hair, his face looked more akin to ground meat than anything remotely resembling a person.

Nova pushed and struggled against the man holding her down as Shanti strolled over and stabbed him in the back with a dagger, just as Alana got up and kicked her captor down. "You'd think you would know better, Kel?" Shanti snarled out as she walked up to him and drove her knee upwards into his groin, leaving him groaning in pain on the floor.

"Please Shanti! One more week… I can't pay you back yet!" Kelvem pleaded as he clung between his legs. Nova felt bad for the agony this male must have been feeling.

Shanti sat on his back, grabbing him by the hair. "And why in the name of the gods can't you, ya slimy pig?" she asked, while digging her heel into his side.

"I lost it! Gambling on fights!" *Slam!* Nova winced, watching as Shanti introduced his face to the floor in a brutish manner. *It must be a great deal of coins to be worth hurting him so much,* Nova thought. Beneath her thought there was an inkling of guilt, yet she found it easy to ignore.

Shanti pulled his head back, his nose disfigured into a flattened and bloodied mess. "Either you find something worth double what you owe me in this lavish shit stain of a mansion of yours, or I take fangs. Alana! Pliers!" Shanti casually held her hand out for the drunken woman to place a tool in her palm.

Then, a *clack, clack, clack* rang out as Shanti squeezed the pliers before spearing them into the man's mouth and yanking a front tooth out, resulting in an eruption of bloody and agonized screams.

Standing up, Shanti kicked him onto his back before straddling his chest. "Nova, come hold his head."

Nova nodded and did as requested. She wondered if Valen would be angry at her for this, but would only offer silent obedience. "My mates! They have priceless jewelry… take it all!" Kelvem groaned out, withholding his sobs as best as he could.

Shanti pushed the pliers into his mouth again. "Hmm, no. I don't think that's enough. Alana, go find his shit."

"Roger tha'!" Alana cheered out as she took off rifling through the various rooms. With a swift yank, Shanti pulled another vampiric fang from Kelvem's mouth, and Nova could even spot pieces of his venom gland as he roared out in agony.

What would Shanti say if she knew that such an act left me sick to my stomach? Nova questioned to herself as she felt her bile rising in her throat and fought to keep it down.

Kelvem groaned out as blood leaked from his mouth. "Fine! You can have it all! Take everything you want until the debt's satisfied! Please, just stop!" With a glob of spit shot at his face, Shanti gestured for Nova to stand with her, and next came the swing of her boot, knocking a dent into Kelvem's skull before she took off to rifle with Alana.

Nova looked down at the unconscious males, and the now dead one who'd tackled her. *Was any amount of gold worth this carnage?* a voice whispered in the back of her mind.

Something about witnessing females like Alana and Shanti, who fought and dominated any in their path, made her envious. She craved to have strength like theirs, so she might defend those in need, and be free from the tyrants still out there. She caught up to Shanti, who was rolling up a painting and stacking it in a pile of others. "How do I become strong… like you and Alana?" Nova questioned as she began looking for shiny things. She did not know what was of value as the office held the similar vainly beautified sense of the Seelie Court. An extravagant surface of trophies, and gold or gems laid about anywhere possible, yet devoid beyond the surface.

"You watch the world burn. Survive, adapt, thrive. The golden rule, don't forget it," Shanti said as she scooped up the paintings and carried them out to see Alana dragging a chest. "You are strong, Nova; far stronger than you give yourself credit for. You've already done the hardest part. Survive. Now put your big bitch pants on and adapt. We'll talk about thriving when you've got your shit together." Shanti's hand came to her shoulder, with a proud curl across her lips, and a source of heat bloomed in Nova's chest, one that made her wish to be unstoppable like Shanti.

I'm strong? I did the hardest part, Nova thought to herself before she fell silent and turned her eyes away. Shanti's mantra echoed in her mind. *Survive, adapt, thrive.* She was lost in thought until Alana yelled out to her. "Lass! C'mere! Am a little tossed right now ta' be pickin' locks." With her front teeth sunk into her bottom lip, Nova kneeled down. "Ya cram these in tha' lock and feel 'round fer tha' pins tha' lift. Bring em up a little till they click, while putin' tension with this one," Alana explained to her as she took the tools offered and eyed them. Curious to learn how such neatly shaped plain strips of copper could unravel locks.

She kneeled down, getting close to it, and she moved the tools into the lock, using one to apply tension as she raked about with the other. At first it was frustrating, as she had such little space to move the tool back and forth, but she found the pins and began picking away.

After lifting the first pin, the tool in her hand bent and she pulled it out, with Alana quick to snatch the pick and hand her another. "Show ya how ta fix it later, lass, aye?" the vampiress said as she gestured for Nova to continue. "Better than stone. Knappin's a pain in tha arse," she grumbled out before taking another drink.

With a resolute nod, she fixated on the lock, sliding the pick in, taking her time, feeling where each pin was until she began lifting them one at a time

Several minutes passed, and with a distinct *click*, she'd unlocked the chest. "I did it!" Nova cheered out as she ripped the lock off and thrust the lid open, revealing what had to be hundreds of vibrantly colored stones with various markings etched into them. They came to the brim of the chest.

"Good, the Rune Coven can pay me on the open contract for these too. Nova and Alana carry the paintings and jewelry. I will grab the chest," Shanti barked out as they left the mansion with their riches in hand, after Shanti had heaved the chest over her shoulder with a husky grunt. "I'll be back later for all the other stuff, after we get you back to Valen," Shanti said, leading them back out into Atlantis.

CHAPTER 6

JUICE AND BREW

Shanti dragged them through winding streets as dusk fell over Atlantis, leading them back to the grand Emporium of the northern markets, lanterns flickering to life along the still bustling stalls. Vendors' barks washed over Nova as lively music drifted through the air. Sweet and spicy aromas mingled – strange incenses, perfumes, and baked goods. The cacophony of bartering, laughter, and instruments vied for her attention against displays of odd trinkets and eye-catching colored wares.

They went down a musty and unkept alley, and Shanti suddenly came to a stop at a decrepit door that looked as if it might crumble off its hinges. After a coded knock, a slit slid open, and eyes peered out before the locks disengaged.

Inside, there were displays of glittering gems, artifacts, and even weapons that pulsed with breath. A wrinkled elf man greeted them, who introduced himself as Galaton, a discreet broker of goods of questionable origin. One by one, Shanti revealed their plundered paintings, rings, and necklaces, and the elf inspected each piece, murmuring at the quality before writing out a list. *That looks hard,* Nova thought while attempting to make sense of what she saw as scribbles.

For an hour, sharp negotiations ensued until they struck deals, and Nova watched wide-eyed as they exchanged spoils for hefty purses of coin.

Be aggressive, like Shanti, in trading, she mused, taking another glimpse of her new life, as she learned to adore each step. The violent parts were unsettling, yet she felt a burning desire to no longer be weak. To be so strong, no one could hurt her, and she could defend those like her, just as Valen had done.

With the last items sold off, and the four purses heavy with gold, the elf smiled. "You ladies bring only the finest as usual, Madam Odin's-Eye, may the All Father guide you until we cross paths again…" With a nod and a farewell, Shanti gathered up their profits and led them back into the lively Atlantean evening. All the wares except the runes were sold off, despite the male's best efforts to get Shanti to part with them. She fixed two of the purses onto her hip and handed the other two to Alana.

"Do I get any coins?" Nova asked as she followed them through the streets.

Shanti looked back at her and patted Nova's back with a heavy hand. "Yes, I'll give it to Valen until you're taught how to barter and not get your gold stolen." They turned into the guild district, and Nova's eyes sought every detail, even if it meant an eventual headache. *Do they not think I am smart enough to handle coins?* she wondered.

"The wrath of the divine is upon us! Foolish, just as our forefathers cast themselves above the Grand Creator, we venerate flesh above spirit!" Nova's attention shot from the street vendors' haggling to a booming voice rising above the clamor. In the middle of the bustling marketplace, standing atop the wood roofed stalls, a man cried out. Though advanced in years, he had a formidable frame. A thick mane of dark curls streaked with gray fell well below his shoulders, restrained by intricate braids. His face was weathered and creased, yet his eyes blazed like twin beacons, as his free hand flailed in a flurry of horror.

"The Deluge cometh!" he said, his voice a deep bellow, as he gestured skyward with his staff. "Repent before the flood waters sweep you away! And the ather is naught more than flame." Nova paused, a chill running down her spine. His eyes were wild, possessed by something that left her chest feeling hollowed out after meeting his gaze. The people continued on ignoring his raving speech, but Nova found herself transfixed. *Was he just mad?* She glanced at the dark clouds looming over the central temples. For a fleeting moment, she wondered if there was truth in his ominous words. But just as quick, the notion passed, the ranting fading into the background clamor of the market. *What does it all mean? No one listened... are gods of Terra wrathful?* She clutched Alana's hand as she noticed her own were slick with sweat, unsure how to process it all. She couldn't take her eyes off him, even if she couldn't make out his shouts.

Next came the Rune Coven, it felt as if they had crossed from one end of Atlantis to another. Nova found her legs beginning to tire just as they came upon a well-adorned guildhall. Masterful stonemasonry littered the facade of the hall. The more Nova stared, the more intricate details she could find. Sigils emanated a variety of colorful and sparkling auras. As they approached the door, it swung open, and a near empty entryway greeted them save for the single woman standing behind a desk, a contraption affixed to her head as she held a stone in one hand and a tool in another.

When they made their way to the desk, Shanti set the chest down atop it with a sharp creak protesting from the wood. With a quick pull, the lid of the chest came open and Shanti revealed the runes. "You sorry fools are looking for these."

The tan skinned witch stuttered at the sight of a chest full of stolen runes when Shanti lifted the chest's lid. "I have to get the Guild Master..." She spoke in a panic before running off, only to come back with a man a finger length shorter than Shanti, wearing colorful robes with elaborate markings across the fabric.

"Esme, you said they have a chest full?" the man said as he and the witch who had greeted them emerged from a door, a brisk hustle getting them down the hall to meet Nova and her new companions. He wore simple robes, with his hair and much of his face obscured by the hood, and a long faded brown beard.

"Yes, Guild Master! It looks like the chest that was stolen from our caravan a month ago." The girl caught her breath as she hunched over.

The Magus stepped forward and offered his hand, which Shanti and Alana shook. "Guild Master Raykon, at your service…?"

"Shanti… Alana, take Nova for grub." Shanti shooed the two of them away.

"Aye lass!" With a hand around her wrist, Alana was dragging Nova out and off to an area full of street vendors selling food. "Ye have fun wit' us, lass?" Alana inquired as she stepped in line for a vendor who served what smelled like heavenly roasted meats.

"Yes! I've learned so much today. Like picking locks, and how to burgle?" Nova spun the ring on her finger, contemplating what to get from the vendor, deciding to get whatever Alana did to learn.

"Tha'd be debt collectin' me dear, close though. Ye should join us? Shanti an' I always be findin' adventures, aye?" Alana's offer came, which sounded so tempting to Nova, yet she wanted to find Valen, to make sure he was okay.

"It sounds tempting. I want to be strong like you and Shanti. I wish I was as strong as Shanti when I was a slave," Nova said, feeling odd when Alana snorted in amusement.

"Lass, ye already're strong. Takes strength ta' keep pushin' through what ye 'ave. We'll find the big lad and make sure everythin's good. If ye wanna join us, we will welcome ye. Shanti enjoys taking wee lassies in need of a good arse kick ta be tha best they can be." Alana stepped to the front of the line and rambled out an order. "Ten shrimp skewers, an' all yer juice." A handful of coins later and Alana was carrying a small, thin-walled satchel full of sticks pointing out of it and she held a jug of strange looking yellow fluids.

Nova followed Alana to a bench and sat beside her, and, once seated, Alana offered her a skewer with the most peculiar looking curved lumps of pink and white meat. "Shrimp? Is it good?"

"Aye! Tha' is me favorite thin' to eat. Nae, much o' it in me homelands. This 'ere is mango juice," Alana said.

She took them from Alana and had a bite of one *shrimp*. The explosion of flavor from the sweet meat and herbs made her smile so wide her cheeks ached, prompting her to squeal with delight. She ate all of her skewers in a frenzy before chugging a portion of the juice, laying back into the bench and finding herself feeling a bulging tension in her belly.

"Yer a hungry lass. Ya eat well, bet in nae time ye'll be fighting males off," Alana said with a snicker as Nova's nose scrunched up in disinterest.

"I… I'm not interested in finding a mate." Her words came out as a low mumble, with furrowed brows at Alana's comment.

"Different stroke fer different folks, aye?" Alana couldn't help but cackle out before dining on her own shrimp, even giving Nova two of them. They then got up and walked around sharing the rest of the juice, which tasted different after Alana poured one of her personal bottles into it and shook it.

"The juice tastes funny…" Nova slurred out as she felt a buzzing sway loose through her body, each step her vision lost.

"Aye, put me brew in it. It'll make ye feel good! Juice and brew is always a good time, lass!" The two wandered around the area, Nova listening to Alana's tales of her and Shanti's exploits as they passed the drink back and forth.

As time passed on and Nova sipped away at the drink, she found a delightful warmth rush over her body, alongside a desire to lean against Alana for comfort. "You're comfy," Nova said under her breath, as she felt a hand come up to her scalp and begin grazing nails along flesh. She exhaled a low breath as her arms wrapped around Alana's waist. *I could die happy right now,* she thought to herself as a low involuntary rumble escaped her chest.

"Gotcha purrin' fer me, lass. Ain't ya a cutie," Alana said, smiling down at Nova. Without a reply to give, Nova shut her eyes and began to drift off against Alana's chest, finding the cool touch of her skin odd yet comforting.

"Fate's fucking sakes! Alana, you got her drunk!" Shanti barked out sometime later, before a clear *thud* came from the heel of her palm, striking the back of Alana's head. With a yank, she pulled both of them to their feet. "I oughta hoof you in the tit, you Scotian bitch."

Nova struggled to stay standing as she swayed about. "I enjoy being… drunk." Nova cheered out as she leaned into Alana, quick to sling an arm around the vampiress for support.

She'd already noted the stark, cool touch of her skin.

"An' tha' lass can handle it well. Seen males drop quicker," Alana said as she pinched Nova's cheek, drawing a shriek of pain from her.

Shanti rolled her eyes before hoisting Nova over her shoulder. "Let's go. We're taking you home. I ain't got the time, patience, or marbles to put up with you like this," Shanti snapped out.

Nova clumsily wriggled, her entire world askew. "Shanti… I can walk!" she whined out until Alana pressed the bottle of juice and brew they'd been drinking to her lips.

"Hush yer gob lass!" Alana said, her voice a light whisper; a tender touch to her cheek with her other hand offering a gentle pour of the *juice*. Nova took two mouthfuls before slumping in defeat across Shanti's back.

"One drunk is enough. We're giving her back to Valen and Ajax. I know one of his places is in the Southern district," Shanti grumbled out as she snatched the bottle from Alana and chugged it before sending it smashing to the ground. "If you keep pissing me off Alana, I'm feeding you to an orca!" she snarled out, with a rueful stomping on the cobblestone ground.

Alana turned pale and silent following behind Shanti, leaving Nova to roll around on Shanti's back giggling in her stupor; that was until Shanti thrust her upon Alana. "Ello lass, ye sounded like ya were havin' a blast, being tossed issa good time aye?" the brunette asked with a warm smile.

Nova giggled and shifted to stand in Alana's arms, only to sway before stumbling. "Aye! I enjoy being tossed!" she said as she caught herself against Alana.

"Don't tempt me!" Shanti grumbled out before her foot connected with the door in front of her, sending it clear off the hinges and tumbling into the darkness.

There wasn't even a moment to react before Shanti had shoved her into the house; an awkward stumble forward, staring out into the pitch-black expanse before her eyes adjusted. "No one's here..." she said in a low whisper.

"No shit. They'll come. Someone will," Shanti replied, walking past her, her shoulder checking a door open that led to an office and dropping her ass into the seat, kicking her feet up onto the desk. "I know how that knife eared fucker thinks," Shanti yawned out, shifting herself into a comfortable position for a nap.

"I have those..." Nova scowled at Shanti's rude remark.

"Cry me a river, Nova. I'll call you a knife eared fucker too!" Shanti grumbled out as she drifted off into slumber.

Alana sat down against the wall with a soft cackle. "Yer a good lass, sit wit' me!" Nova stumbled toward Alana and complied, leaning into her shoulder. "Ye know yer hair is tha prettiest thin've ever seen!" Alana pushed a hand into Nova's dense mass of blue hair, causing her to snuggle up closer.

"Zip your booze hole Alana! I'm taking a nap!" Shanti

shouted out as she kicked her boot off to collide with the wall beside Alana's head, causing her to stifle Nova's laughter.

Footsteps approaching startled Nova awake, and she looked at Alana, as her earthy brown eyes peeled wide and focused on the door, with a glance behind her in horror to see that Shanti was still sleeping.

The door swung open and there stood Ajax in elegant tailored robes. The look on his face was unamused as he approached Shanti. With a simple flick of his finger, he grounded her feet and cleaned his entire desk with a wave of dark purple magic. "Must you disturb my dwellings every time we share the same locale? It's a rather ostentatious habit of attention seeking." Ajax locked gaze with Shanti; the two facing off with one another, each still, as if frozen in place. A silent war between the two of them filled the air.

"Yes. The blue-haired lost lamb, she's Valen's, correct?" Shanti grumbled out while toeing her other boot off before placing her feet back on his desk.

Valen, who was following closely behind Ajax, moved toward Nova and scooped her up. "Not mine. Free." Nova squirmed to snuggle as close to his heated chest as she could, his reminder of her freedom making her heart pound against her chest.

"Yeah, yeah, big guy. Go take her to bed. We've got business to discuss." With a dramatic wave, Shanti banished them.

Nova was happy to be reunited with Valen, the radiant warmth that emanated from him soothing her after a long day. "Thank you, Shanti," Valen spoke before he left the room with Nova, whisking her off to her own bedroom. She clutched at his tunic, hoping it would keep him from putting her down.

"Have good day?" he asked as his one free hand ran through her hair.

"Uh-huh…" Nova let out before drifting off in his arms, only to be brought back to the world of the waking when he began lying her down in bed.

"Can I stay with you tonight? I don't want to sleep alone… and I missed you." After a moment of contemplation, Valen had her in his embrace once more and he moved to his own room. The size of his bed was bewildering; it looked like four of her own. Once she was under the covers, and he moved out of sight to his private washroom, she bit her lip. Waiting for his return was an endeavor of patience.

Why is he so kind to me? I've not done anything to deserve it, a voice in the back of her mind whispered.

Valen returned wearing only a pair of lush cotton pants, his massive chest on display. Scars, faded tattoos, and a dense thicket of hair covered his torso. It amazed her how silently he moved as he slipped under the covers beside her.

She curled up against his chest, being tickled by the curly hairs yet lulled to sleep by his heat, and his hand running through her hair. The last thing she could recall before slumber captured her was him shifting to curl his large body around her, as if to shield her from potential danger. *Safety*, was her final thought before sleep overtook her.

CHAPTER 7

CALL OF FATE

Narrowly opening her eyes as she awoke, Nova let out a soft groan and stretched her legs out to be reminded that Valen enveloped her with the most comforting warmth. The giant beside her was fast asleep as she sat up, looking over at him. Part of her craved to curl up in the bed beside him for the rest of her life, but something in her gut beckoned for more. For more. For more. Her time with Valen was assuredly short, which made her heart sink into a pit she didn't know existed.

Leaning down, she pressed her lips to the rough texture of his cheek and laid back down to nestle herself against him once more. It might not be her fate, but she would enjoy his kindness while she had it. Her mind wandered to imagining the blessed female to be his compassion. She imagined someone small and fragile; even more in need of him than herself.

Lying there, unable to sleep, she racked her mind, toying with Alana's offer and learning how to be indomitable like Shanti. Contemplating if that was the life she had to seek. The idea of living from one adventure to another excited her, seeing the world she had no clue about.

Hopefully, even exploring the lost courts of the fae, and finding the truth to her mother's tales. Her eyes drifted to the ring on her finger that in this moment weighed so incredibly heavy. *I am the only one who can bring the light of the Moon Court back.* She needed those with the strength she wished to find in herself, which meant demanding Shanti take her on as an apprentice.

With a final nuzzle to Valen's chest, she got to her feet and tiptoed about the room, noting every detail where each item would be and, knowing Valen, she imagined he wouldn't move a thing until she returned. Sitting atop the vanity was a smooth jade the size of her palm, yet thinner than a gold coin. A piece of paper sat under it. A series of drawings. His clever way of depicting that the stone was for her by drawing a small crudely sketched version of himself, handing the stone to a patiently labored doodle of herself. She made a mental reminder to pick up the stone while moving to the door and paused, taking one last glance at Valen, whose amber gaze caught her own. She gave him a silent wave as she turned her back to him, a small smile curling across his lips that left her emboldened that she was making the right choice.

She followed the scent of what she recalled matched Alana,

knowing she'd be near Shanti.

Soon she found herself in the kitchen bombarded with a horrific stench of cooking. Alana grinned wildly as she slurped up some of her rancid dish. "G'mornin lass! Ye wan' some haggis? Very good, an' healthy dish o' me motherland!" the vampiress said, offering a spoonful to her. The closer it came, the more tears stung Nova's eyes. *How does she eat that?* Nova wondered, as she nearly tripped on her own feet, reeling back.

"I wouldn't. It's all the garbage parts of a sheep cooked in its own stomach." Shanti's voice rang out from the small dining room.

"Ah… no thank you Alana… I wanted to talk to Shanti," Nova uttered, before slipping into the dining room where Shanti and Ajax sat, documents and maps strewn across the table.

"What Nova? Ajax and I are talking business," Shanti snapped out without even looking at her, only sticking a forkful of raw meat into her mouth and keeping her eyes fixed on the document she'd been reading.

"I want you to train me to be like you! I don't care where we go or what we do. Show me how to become tough like you." Nova stood firm as she spoke out without mincing a single word.

A cruel grin crossed the lycaness' lips as she pushed to her feet. "Are you sure about that, Nova? You saw what we did yesterday." Nova gave a nervous nod of the head as her eyes went to Ajax. He sat content to silently watch how it played out. "Use your words," Shanti grumbled out as her arms crossed her chest with a disapproving glare to her eyes.

"Yes! I want this. I don't care how hard it is. Train me to be strong like you!" Nova shouted out. Shanti returned to her seated position and leaned back, gesturing for Nova to come close. She complied, and Shanti's hands came up to Nova's cheeks as she kneeled next to her.

"You might die. Are you ready for that?" Shanti's question wormed its way into her soul.

A taste of death was something she once experienced daily. Nova's coppery eyes drifted down to her mother's ring before looking back up at Shanti. "I care not if I die, for I've yet to truly live. There's nothing for me to lose," she uttered without a thought, feeling herself exposed before the shrewd eyed duo before her. Ajax's gaze remained curious through the entire discussion.

With a pat on her head, Shanti focused back on Ajax. "Good, we're going to need you, anyway. Ya weren't getting a choice. Ajax and you need to work on your magic, as Alana and I don't have any being a lycan and a vampire. Just learn the basics. After that, Alana and I will take you with us. I'll be your mentor. Rest up today because starting tomorrow Ajax will train you," Shanti said as she pegged Nova with an almost endearingly maternal gaze that left her feeling disoriented.

"You will have three days to learn magic, Nova. After that I must return to my affairs. Once you embark with Shanti and Alana, there will be no turning back, not until your job is complete," Ajax said while lifting a dainty, pure white steaming cup to his lips. The scent of the herbaceous brew reminded her of the teas the Seelie King drank.

"What is the job?" Nova fiddled with the ring impatiently, feeling as if she were about to burst.

Shanti slapped her own thigh and howled out, "That's the kinda gumption I like to see!"

Ajax waved dismissive gesture at Shanti, drawing Nova's attention. "An artifact buried deep within the heart of the Feywilds. I wish to confirm its existence and determine how useful or dangerous it might prove to be. If the legends are true, it is an artifact created by the combined might of the angels and dragons, created for the very Moon Goddess your mother venerated. They cannot pursue this without you." With the tap of his hand to a detailed map of areas of the Feywilds, he continued, "It goes beyond any charted territory. I cannot say for certain what trials await you, but if you survive, you will come out of this a different person than you are today." Ajax settled the cup down and leaned forward in his seat. "You seem rather content with Valen and Atlantis. Are you prepared to let that go? The first comfort in your life, only to walk away from it. I would not fault you for wishing to stay."

"I adore the comfort he provides, but it's not what fate wants of me. I don't wish to be weak any longer… I can seek it when I come back!" Nova said, as she looked over the maps. With a sigh, she looked at Ajax. It was terrifying to match his gaze, but she had to, in order to prove how determined she was.

"Nova'ivar, you've never been weak. You survived the

cruelty of a Seelie prince. That demands strength far beyond what Shanti holds from being a brute." His cold amethyst eyes bored into her, only for her to see a glimmer of warmth beneath the icy exterior of the villainous myth of a male before her. "Do you understand? Never consider yourself anything less, for within is a force that brings kingdoms to a kneel." His words came at her, leaving an imprint in her mind, just as Shanti's mantra had.

Nova nodded and, moved to his side to hug him. "Thank you for freeing me and fighting the prince." She gave him a firm squeeze only to find his temperature fluctuated rapidly.

A brief chuckle came from Ajax before he nudged her away, not one for physical affection. "That wasn't my doing. That would be Syphr, my Shadow. Syphr show yourself," Ajax said before a male, one head taller than Ajax and Shanti appeared from thin air, long silvery hair running down the length of his back as he sported armor that itself looked like pure darkness taken form.

With a bow at the hip, Syphr presented himself, pale and sunken in eyes, staring at her. In this moment, she felt as if her eyes were staring into an endless abyss, as awe-inspiring as it was fear inducing. Nova stepped toward this male, and she leaned forward pushing herself up to wrap her arms around his neck. "Thank you for defending me, Syphr. I hope I can repay the debt one day!" she said, giving him the tightest squeeze she could muster, when two thin arms gently enclosed around her, and she froze up before leaning into him.

The pressure in Syphr's embrace was the faintest of touches, and she turned her eyes upward to look at his face as a whisper of a voice left his lips. "It was right," he said, his voice an empty echo that sent a shiver up her spine.

Nova listened before she stepped back, pondering everything. She smiled at Syphr and gave him a nod. "I hope when the time comes, I do the right thing." With that, Syphr slipped away into the shadows as Nova settled at the table and listened in on the planning of the expedition.

"What is the artifact?" she asked after countless silent minutes of taking in every detail they discussed – each individual item Shanti needed and why, even an exchange of bags of gold for her.

Ajax sifted through the scattered pages and held one up. It was an intricate drawing of a pair of copper rings. One ring matched the one that now fit more snug around her finger with the food and rest of recent days. "You already have one. One of the final times I last spoke with Sela'mann, she said the other High Priestess stayed during the Unseelie assault on the Court of Moon to during the fall the complete set could never fall into the wrong hands."

"How do you know wild fae haven't already taken them?" Nova stared at her ring, wondering just what power she had had all these centuries.

Ajax's fingers slipped around hers, causing an involuntary rush of heat to her cheeks, before he moved to yank her ring off her finger, only for a burst of light to thrust him off his seat and onto the floor. "That enchantment remains even in death, according to Sela. Only living descendants of the Moon

Goddesses may carry them out of the Court." He moved back to his seat after brushing himself off with a snap and shimmer of magic.

Shanti pointed to a cave entrance mapped out. "Vyz's Passage, let's take that to the far north. That is the fastest route without having to cut through swamps, and deal with the muck," she said.

"If you think that's the route you'll take, then feel free. I would advise while we train Nova, that we each scout about to ensure you have the best path laid out for the first leg of your expedition," Ajax said as he began gathering up the papers into organized piles.

Shanti stood up and began pacing around the room. "Yes, that's smart. The Feywilds likes to play tricks and change things up on ya," she said as she stepped into the kitchen, only to send something flying at Nova.

A leather bag hit her head, causing Nova to yelp out. "Hey! What was that for?" She sneered at Shanti as the tall female stepped before her.

"Carrying your shit," Shanti said, before plopping back down into her seat.

Nova eyed the bag and noted its construction, as she gathered its design was to be affixed around her hips. Sizeable enough for bare necessities. "Will this be my only bag?"

"You carry what you bring. I ain't hoofing anything extra but my foot in your ass!" Shanti barked out, before letting out a brief cackle in amusement toward herself.

I can't bring much then. Maybe Valen can show me what I need, she mused, hoping a second shopping adventure would go more smoothly.

The talks continued, though, and they began to feel repetitive between Shanti and Ajax; one questioning the other's ideas or input, and then a difficult debate ensuing that became hard to follow.

CHAPTER 8

MEMORIES AND GEAR

Hours passed as Nova sat there listening to Ajax and Shanti bickering over the impending expedition for the Moon Court, and she pondered the tales her mother had passed down to her, finding herself lost in memory.

She ran through the seemingly endless hedge maze near the Seelie Palace, happy to have a day outside the castle, away from her tedious chores. Her fingertips poked through the multi-colored leaves, until a thorn pricked her finger. She pulled it free from the shrubbery wall and silently watched as a red trickle appeared at the tip. She didn't hesitate and quickly inserted her finger into her mouth, and a moment later, the dull ache faded.

A tall woman with hair matching her own, but skin as pale as the Moon, appeared beside her and scooped her up. "Nova'ivar, my darling little rascal, we came out here for a picnic since his majesty permitted us an afternoon away!" her mother said with a playful scolding, drawing her upwards for a kiss to the cheek, as Nova wriggled herself free and settled on the ground.

Sela'mann recited words of a forgotten tongue right before an entire picnic spread appearing from thin air. "There we are. I spoke with the chef to get us trimmings, and he gave us an entire steak!" Sela handed Nova her covered dish with the steak neatly cut into cubes.

"He must think you're pretty." Nova took the dish and placed it in her lap. "Thank you, Mama! Can you tell me about our old court again?" she asked as she popped a cube of meat into her mouth.

Sela gave Nova a coy grin at her compliment before uncovering her own dish. "Ah... the Moon Court. What would you like to know?" she asked as she ate pieces of her own meat.

"Was it beautiful?" Nova inquired as she stopped eating to focus on her mother.

Sela gave a nod and held her hand out, an elaborate spectacle of light burst forth, showing the intricate designs of a temple dedicated to the three Moons. Buwan, Galach, and Tungl. "The most beautiful at one point, I was the Grand Priestess of Buwan. This was my home until a group of the Unseelie Court's charmed vampires and shifters invaded. Few of us fled to the Seelie Court, and as you know, the prince took a liking to me and I've been in his care since." Sela held up a kerchief to dab at Nova's messy face.

"Can we go back to our Court?" Nova asked as she sipped from the waterskin filled with juice her mother brought along. "No, sadly not. When I awoke in the Seelie Court after falling ill during the journey, I was told only six of us survived and we were all servants to members of the royal family. Perhaps I might convince Prince Rys to allow us to convene to celebrate a festival of Buwan. She will be full soon after all." Sela's voice drifted to a solemn edge, only for her tone to shift into a higher spirited one. Already done with her food, she laid back against the grass and sighed. "I will speak to him when we get back. The festival ends with someone gaining Buwan's blessing, a sign of greatness." Nova listened intently as she scarfed down her food and then curled up atop her mother's lap.

"Who received the last blessing?" She let out a long drawn-out yawn, drifting off to the story of the young fae boy who was a member of the survivors, who now was the proud mate of a lesser princess in the Court.

She was nearly asleep when her mother pinched her nose gently, all the while cooing out, "It isn't nap time."

Nova grumbled, sitting up and rubbed at her face. "Mama, can we race back to the palace? I've been practicing!" Nova said, as her mother snapped, summoning magic to tidy their picnic.

"Is that so?" Sela stood up, before uttering a whisper of ancient words, sending the basket soaring through the air toward the kitchen entrance. "Ready yourself Nova. If you lose, you get to scrub the dishes!" She crudely stuck her tongue out at Nova

after her challenge, something they were only allowed to do when they were outdoors.

Nova presented her own back and jumped up to her feet, bracing herself to run. She took a deep breath and her own magic shrouded her body, channeling toward her legs. "Go!" Nova shouted before taking off, winding through the maze to the exit.

The rush of wind against her face, and heart throbbing, had her giggling with glee. Her mother hadn't caught up, which had her feeling motivated to win. Upon exiting the maze, she pushed ahead toward the bridge that led to the palace, passing through the gap between the bridge guards as a blur. A burning swept through her legs and yet she continued her fixation of mana..

The palace entrance was directly in sight, its elegant ivory arches and spires greeting her home. She pushed harder, flooding all the magic she could to her feet, as her mother appeared behind her. Instead of running, Sela glided across through the ather, effortlessly moving alongside her as they neared the end of the bridge. "You have gotten quicker darling!" Sela's voice rang out from beside her as they neared the steps.

Nova took one last look at the endless gardens and hedge maze. She'd always imagined sneaking out at night to wander the gardens alone. To pick one of every flower for a bouquet she might present to the King. A soothing warmth, along with a presence next to her, drew her from her memories.

Nova stirred from her trance when she felt Valen beside her. She wished she could return to those simple days. Shanti and Ajax were wrapping up their conversation as Valen ate a plateful of the hazardously scented dish Alana had prepared.

His expression showed he was less than pleased with it, but his polite nature got the best of him. "Good morning, Valen!" Nova greeted him cheerfully as she leaned into him, wondering if he could join them.

"Good morning, Nova." Valen brought a tender hand against her cheek, and she couldn't resist nuzzling herself into his warmth.

"Valen, please take Nova to buy new clothes. She'll be joining Shanti in the Feywilds. We will make final arrangements before we head to the Ether." Ajax stood up and left with Shanti, while Alana was busy eating her food, cleaning the kitchen, and bellowing with what she assumed was joyous misery.

Valen cleaned up after himself, handing his plate to Alana before returning to Nova's side. She stood up and moved with him toward the door, taking his hand in her own. "Do you think you could come with us? I'm scared to go to the Feywilds…"

"We ask Ajax. Maybe?" he offered Nova as they headed into a small seamstress' boutique. They only left with six pairs of underwear. It took three different boutiques before she found a leather jacket she liked, and with it she bought a thick cotton tunic that had buttons she could do and undo at her own comfort, and even a sturdy pair of boots that came up to the upper part of her calves. She stared at herself in the mirror; she was fond of her new outfit. Proudly, she stepped out from the dressing rooms, her fists at her hips confidently.

Valen was writing in a journal when his focus turned on her, and he gave her a nod. "Look good. Durable. Comfy!" He got up and stuffed his journal away then paid the merchant a stack of gold and silver coins.

"Should I get a weapon?" she wondered aloud as she let Valen lead her through the city. It felt wonderful just being in such a new domain, the heady scent of industry all around them.

"Yes. Know good smiths," Valen replied as the *clanging and banging* of hammers striking metal came into earshot. Artisans of every craft filled the entire district of the city, and Nova curiously peeked into every open stall. That was until they came to a door that was tall enough for Valen to walk through without ducking his head. Between the noise and all the harsh scents that filled the air, she was unsure which was the worse pollutant.

The sight of seven dwarves was unexpected. Four of them swung hammers at a length of red-hot metal in a rhythmic series of *clangs and bangs*, a fifth polished a chest plate, while the sixth shaped the edge of a blade, and the seventh was hunched over a ledger and a pile of coins. "G'day, what can I do for ya?" the dwarf scribbling into a book questioned.

Valen tapped Nova's back, nudging her toward the desk. "I need a weapon…" She peered at the ledger despite her inability to read.

The mountain of coins and Valen's word meant a great deal to her. "What kind? Spear? Sword? Axe? Go look at our stock," the bookkeeper said with a lazy gesture toward the wall of weapons.

Nova stepped toward the wall and eyed the large array of weapons. There were blades ranging from slim and short knives to swords that looked unwieldy even for Valen. She took a saber the length of her arm into her hands and waved for Valen to join her. "Do you think this one is good?" Nova maneuvered it around, careful to avoid coming near Valen with the edge.

"How sword feel? All weapons Seven make great." Valen lifted a massive axe, stepping toward the training dummy, bisecting it with one mighty cleave. The dummy pulled back with an array of vibrant orange and dark grey magic glowing at the sliced ends, drawing it together as if he had never split it in two.

Nova raised the saber for a slash only to find the blade stuck in the dummy, and Valen yanked it free and shook his head. "Not right," he said, while slipping the weapon from her hands, quick to replace it with a spear.

"Spear simple. Try." Valen pulled a larger spear from the wall and showed how to use it by burying the tip into the dummy with a swift thrust forward.

With his weapon freed, Nova took a stab at the dummy, her hand now aching. The grip felt too robust for her. "I don't like the way it feels. Maybe something smaller?" she asked as her eyes studied the different shapes of weapons, wondering why there was such a wide variety of tools solely designed to hurt others.

"How 'bout ya try a dagger?" the dwarf that had been defining the edge on a sword before asked, now standing at her side. *His hat looks like Shanti's boot*, Nova mused to herself as he pointed to a dagger on the wall.

"I thought dwarves were all gone?" Nova asked as she took the straight edged dagger and looked over the shining copper.

"We just ain't in yer fancy courts. Most came to Terra, the rest sought ancestral grounds," one dwarf, swinging a hammer, said aloud before dropping the hammer onto the red-hot metal they'd been working, his lengthy, braided gray beard and hair flying wildly with each swing.

"I'm about to do that!" Nova said as she took a clumsy slash at the dummy, nearly falling on her face, saved only by Valen's swift reflexes.

"Ain't yer ancestral grounds the Courts?" the polisher asked, turning his focus toward Nova and slowing his motions, as she wondered to herself what the contraption of metal and glass was covering his eyes.

"Not the Seelie Court, my mother is from the Court of Moons." Nova switched daggers to a narrower one between words.

"Ah, they were a good bunch, saved our skins when the Unseelie hunted us. Good bunch. Splains yer hair and eyes." The sharpener stopped in his motions and stared upward in reminiscence, as he set the blade he'd been working on down.

Nova stood at the wall of blades and began picking up and putting down different ones, taking a moment with each to slash and stab with it. "I can't find one that feels right…" she conceded disappointedly, a dejected sigh underscoring her words.

"Ye'll find something. If nothing we have fits yer hand, we can smith anything!" another of the ones swinging a hammer belted out cheerily.

Nova turned to Valen, locking her gaze on his glimmering amber eyes. "Take break. Maybe exotic weapons?" His hand came to pat her shoulder.

Nova went to his side and took his hand. "Yes! I need a drink… can we find juice?" she asked. Valen's nod had her smiling.

"Come again Valen, we ought ta be done with yer new axe next week." one of the Seven shouted out; Nova was unsure which.

"Thank you," Valen said before leading Nova out of the shop to a juice vendor down the road. The vendor began preparing Nova's drink as a sound caught her ear.

At first, she thought it was just the wind, but the clear beckon of whispers was calling from an alleyway. "Valen, I'm going to look at something. I'll be right back!" Nova said, before slipping away.

She walked into the alley, where trash lined both walls of the buildings, and she settled at the end, where three walls boxed her in. She puffed her cheeks up in frustration, and a startled yelp left her lips when she turned on her heel to leave, and Syphr suddenly stood there. Pale skin like her mother's, with a long mane of silver hair, and eyes that had her stomach tightening with dread. "Mayhap this is for you." He presented the Ethereum dagger that once belonged to the prince. The clear crystal blade had always drawn her eye, and she reached out to take it, the weight feeling perfect against her palm.

"Syphr… where did you get this?" she asked with narrowed eyes.

"The prince's remains," Syphr said, as if taking things from the dead was an everyday occurrence for him.

Nova's brows scrunched up in confusion as she ran her fingers across the flat of the blade. "Valen burned him alive…" she said defensively.

"Valen's flames are not hot enough to destroy Ethereum. Take it," Syphr said in one breath. In the next, he was gone… one with the shadows as always. Holding the dagger toward the sun, Nova witnessed the warm orange rays filtering through, casting a small yet vivid display of colors, as she thought back to the myths of Ethereum, wondering if there was truth behind the need to bond with weapons and items made from the crystal. She pressed her thumb against the bolster and dragged her flesh up to the tip, yanking her hand back at the pain; the trail of her own blood running up the blade absorbing into the edge, as a dark red line ran along the center of the blade. The handle changed shape in her grip, molding itself to match her fingers, and with a quick motion, she sliced through the air, finding the movement effortless, as if the blade were near weightless now. She stuck her thumb in her mouth, sucking at her blood until the wound mended.

She bolted out of the alley to Valen and explained what happened. "Be careful. Need sheath," Valen said, as he handed her drink to her. A slurp at the lip of the cup and she felt refreshed by the yellow fruity taste splashing withing her mouth. "Do you think those dwarves have one?" Nova mused hopefully, a renewed spark lighting up her eyes.

After a quick stop to buy a sheath from the dwarves, she walked through the streets with Valen. She found it peculiar that the dagger was weightless in hand, but at her hip she could feel it. "What sort of gear do you think I should bring? Shanti gave me a bag." She pointed to the bag on her hip.

"Small bag. Travel light easier." Valen led her to another store. It had a simple, plain wooden exterior. The wood itself looked aged and worn, but still firm. She tipped her head to Valen in a silent thanks when he held the door for her before entering. A human man with dull brown hair and eyes, along with a slightly pudgy face, stood behind the counter. "Good day Valen, a new friend?" he asked as the two of them stepped up to the counter.

"Good day. Nova. Gerron," Valen said before taking out a pen and paper to make a list.

Nova eyed the shop, seeing it had many odds and ends, from trinkets of what she assumed were some of the many gods Terrans prayed to, to blemished and battered jewelry, and even waterskins, small daggers, and rolls of paper she imaged were anything from maps of the land to documents of great importance. "He's helping me find travel gear. Your shop is quite homely. You have many things!" She turned her focus to the man. Even though his eyes weren't striking like some of her comrades, he held a kindness; one that she imagined belonged to a loving father.

"Thank you, madam, my brothers travel the world to bring things back to our humble shop." The shop keep bowed his head politely to Nova before Valan handed him the list and he took off to the back.

Moments later, he came out with everything in hand. A needle and thread, flint and steel, and a small sheathed knife. "Here you are, Valen. It'll be five silvers."

Valen was quick to place the silver down, and they departed with a quick farewell. As they began walking back to Ajax's and Valen's, he took out the thread and began showing her how to set it up. He then held out a part of one of his furs and was quick to display lacing the thread and needle to stitch something, then came his method of unraveling it. "No magic? Make fire." He took the flint and steel striking them together spraying vibrant orange shards slicing through the air.

"Is that not magic itself?" she asked as she took the simple tool and struck her own burst of sparks. She couldn't understand how it wasn't magical.

Valen shook his head as he held up the knife. "Magic special… unsure how explain," he said as he unsheathed the small blade and showed her how it would slice a piece of one of his thick furs slung across his shoulders. "Not need dagger always. Precision nice." He tucked the knife into her pouch. "Not need much. Teach how survive off land."

"Thank you for taking me out today, Valen!" Nova nestled herself into his warm side for a hug.

"My pleasure," he said with a gruff smile directed down at her. Her cheeks flushed red as they came up to the door to the house, and the massive male patted his hand against the top of her head before opening the door. "Go meet Ajax. In office." Valen pointed to the door that she assumed she was to go through, and she gave him one last hug and ran off toward it.

⁕⸻❦⸻⁕

Nova stepped into the office, surrounded by scrolls and books on every wall, and a large, dark wooded desk and the back of a chair greeted her. A small portal snapping shut caught her eye, before Ajax spun around in his elegant seat. "Ah, there you are, Nova." A pair of dainty white cups appeared on the desk with wisps of steam and an herbaceous scent coming from them. "Have tea with me. I would like to give you something."

Nova took the seat in front of Ajax, lifting her cup to her lips. "Thank you. It smells wonderful!" Nova said, before taking a sip.

"I see Syphr gave you the prince's dagger. It looks good at your hip," Ajax said.

Nova smiled and pulled the dagger out, laying it on the table. "I've always wanted to hold it," she mumbled.

"You've made your bond with it, I see. Now it is yours until fate claims your soul." Ajax put his cup down and reached into a jacket, setting out a vibrantly colorful crystalline disc before her as he asked, "Do you know what this is?" Nova shook her head, swallowing the tea in her mouth and putting her cup on the saucer.

"It's really pretty, but no," she admitted shamefully, hanging her head.

"Draconite. It is imperative you keep this on you." Ajax's voice was firm, catching her attention before she could fall into sulking over not knowing.

"Why?" Nova asked as she picked up the coin-shaped crystal.

"Just do as I say. It is easier if you listen than I explain. All will make sense in time," Ajax said as he leaned back into his seat, tea in hand.

"You haven't led me astray yet… how would you hide it?" Nova said confidently, and pocketed the draconite.

Ajax sat silently for several long moments before locking his gaze with hers. "Where no one else can find it, *close at hand*," he said with an edge to his words. She gave a nod and looked away to allow a stillness between them fill the air as they each quietly sipped their tea.

Nearly through her cup, she looked at Ajax with a question burning in her mind. "Can you teach me how to read?" Nova mused hopefully as she finished her tea.

With a canter to his head in curiosity he said, "Of course, but why do you wish to learn?"

"Well, I've always wanted to know. I don't remember the little my mother taught me growing up," Nova said, as she fiddled with her fingers nervously.

Ajax snapped his fingers, and a scroll laid itself out across the side of the desk. "Would you like to learn now?" He waved her over.

"Yes, please!" she said, trying to contain her excitement while she moved her seat closer to Ajax and the scroll.

Two hours passed, and Nova now understood the basics of reading as she got up from the desk. "Thank you so much, Ajax!" She flashed her most dazzling smile.

"Why, of course, Nova. Reading is the single most important skill, seconded only by writing. You have been a wonderful companion to share tea with. I will see you in the morning, when we enter the Ether tomorrow find me in the meadow." Ajax said as they stood up and he led her to the door.

Now on her own, she headed to the bathroom; a bath all she could think of. With the water running, she undressed and pulled the draconite from her pocket, Ajax's words echoing in her mind. At first, she'd thought just keeping it in her pocket would be fine, but then her mind raced with the possibilities of how it might get lost being in her pants or pouch.

Close at hand was the only bit of Ajax's guidance, she recalled, as if he'd given her the answer as gruesome as it may sound. Nova reached out for her pile of clothes and gear.

She pulled her dagger free from its sheath, finding only one idea of how to keep the crystal in her possession at no risk of loss, and she dragged the tip of the blade against the meaty part of her palm, clenching her teeth through the pain.

Nova watched the blood run along her arm and drip off her

elbow to the floor before pushing the small draconite disc into her own flesh. Tears leaked from her eyes as the pain brought her to her knees. She fought the urge to cry out, knowing it would alert Valen, as she drew the cut to her lips and let her saliva heal the wound then hurried to clean the dark red splashes across the marble so she might enjoy her bath and quiet evening.

CHAPTER 9

RETURNING TO THE ETHER

Nova's newfound path in life imbued her with a fresh sense of bravado. Her new blade and ensemble of gear inspired her to embrace whatever the future held. She felt like an entirely different female from the one she had been a couple of evenings prior. That was until Ajax snapped open a rift to the edge of the Ether, causing her heart to pound erratically as if it dropped next to her stomach. She was stuck in place with fear, her palms dripping with sweat, her mouth unbearably clammy.

"Move your ass!" Shanti shouted, grabbing her by the seat of her pants and back of her shirt and sending her flying through the rift. A startled yelp escaped her lips as she flew out of the other end and tumbled into the dirt.

Valen was the only one who hadn't kept going, as he knelt beside her, ready to help her up.

Taking his hand, she stood up, a dizzying sensation rushing between her ears. "Thank you Valen." Her voice came out in a frustrated burst as she brushed herself off while walking beside him. "Have you ever been to the Feywilds?" Nova asked, her eyes tracing the rolling hills of wildflowers expelling miasmas of green and red. Valen nodded.

"Twice," he said, gesturing for her to walk faster.

Nova furrowed her brow feeling puzzled by his statement, as she moved her legs quicker to match his gait. "Why did you go?" she asked, her eyes catching sight of a beast in the distance. It was standing above the trees with lengthy, shaggy pink fur.

"One personal journey. One hunt with Shanti," he said before falling silent again, his eyes drawn away from her. She felt it was enough to have gotten this much from him, as she always found a certain charm in his brief way with words, even if it left her with more questions than she had originally. *Maybe he wants me to learn on my own?* she wondered.

Moments later, a small, lonesome cabin made of purple wooded timber came into view, where Alana and Shanti prepared the campsite a dozen paces away.

She knew Ajax wanted her to find him once they got to the cabin, so she quickly hugged Valen's side before taking off in search of him. She found him a mere hundred steps away in a lush meadow that lit up with the most vibrant shades of every color, the ground itself feeling as if it were beating like a heart, and the air sent a numbing buzz across her skin, reminding her of Alana's *brew*.

"Ah, there you are, Nova. Come here." He beckoned to her, and she caught up with him and hunched over to catch her breath. "You could have walked. I am in no rush. Magic demands patience." Ajax shook his head, with a faint grin revealing a hint of play to the scolding.

"I didn't want to waste your time!" She stood up straight, her cheeks slightly reddened. Despite his kindness, Ajax's presence made her heart race and palms run slick, as if he eyed her like a mighty hungry beast.

"Do not fret. We have all the time we need. Tell me, what magic do you know?" Ajax settled on the colorful stump of a once monumental mushroom, like those nearby with their sprouting and spotted caps.

"I only knew my mother. She was the last Grand Priestess of Buwan." Nova tugged at her own sleeve, as Ajax's amethyst eyes fixated on her, causing her to avert her gaze from him as she spun her mother's ring on her finger.

"Ah yes Sela, she was a rare female. One of the last who truly lived by the old ways," Ajax said, his normally shrewd stare softening to a tender gaze. "I knew your mother. She and I had a difficult history. Her fate a common musing of mine," Ajax said, pondering the nostalgia while staring longingly off into the distance.

"I don't remember…" she admitted, bowing her head

shamefully. She had spent ages racking her mind for a memory she couldn't seem to recall.

"My most sincere condolences, Nova. Your mother was a spirit that fate only frees once. I see her beauty and savagery in your eyes." Ajax's hand gently pressed against her back, and she could tell that this was not a gesture he made casually. It held significance.

"Thank you… she only taught me basics." She turned her eyes toward him as he held his hand out.

He offered her a charming grin. "Your mother was an Enchantress," he said as she stilled herself to focus every ounce of her being on him to portray the very might she wished to emulate.

Her eyes turned to Ajax's hand as the energy within the air pulled toward his fingertips. "An Enchantress can embed magic into objects and people with a purpose. Binding and unbinding are second nature. It is a non-combative magic, yet so many rely on it. Step back, please," Ajax said before pulling out an crystal knife with a dragon's talon like curve to the blade and handle, wielding it in a reverse grip. "Only a skilled Enchanter may use ethereum to its true capacity."

With an elegant sway to his hands, Ajax stood and drew the knife close to his midsection, running his fingers along the spine, gathering the magic from around them and within him to flood the once clear crystalline blade with a swirl of ever-changing color.

A dark, ominous purple glow erupted from the blade as he sliced through the air, shooting out and cutting into the base of a massive tree at the edge of the meadow. Ajax's magic ran up the tree, splitting it into equal length segments, with every branch being cleared from the trunk as the purple energy raced to the top. With the last bolt of light, the entire tree fell into a neat stack of logs. "What do you know of ethereum, Nova?"

Her eyes lowered to the ring cradling her finger, and a sudden sense of approval and trust came out of nowhere, easing her shoulders, and reminding her of when she used to explore the arts as a child and her mother would always encourage her best efforts and show pride in anything she made. "I know little… only that it is the second most powerful conduit for magic. The first being draconite, like the piece you gave me." She ran finger tips against the slight bulge in the meat of her palm.

"That is a suitable answer. I've heard much worse from those more educated. Do you know where we stand?" Ajax asked. Nova's eyes scanned the meadow before she shook her head.

"Near the Feywilds…?" She found herself puzzled. *Does he take me for a fool?* she wondered as she crossed her arms over her chest.

A soft chuckle came from Ajax as he held the blade out to her. "You're not wrong. We stand at a node. Every Court, including the lost ones, lives atop major nodes of power. A node comes where at least seven ley lines cross and remain for a thousand years. Come now, bury your blade in the ground." He knelt down, gesturing for her to join him, uncaring that his majestic robes were getting stained on the vibrantly colored grass.

Without hesitation, she followed his instruction, burying her blade till the hilt pressed into muted orange soil. "Now hold on to it. Feel the heart of the Ether itself." He held his hand out to her. She took his hand and together they wrapped their fingers around the blade.

Just as he'd said, there was a rhythmic beat rising from the blade, shooting through her body; power unlike anything she'd felt before. It made even a fae King seem paltry. In this moment, she felt every living being within dozens of miles; every nerve in her body electrified. As she tried to pull away, Ajax's hand held her tight to the handle.

"Do not let go Nova. You must imprint yourself upon the blade and learn what magic you possess. The node is cleaning you and the blade of all magic that isn't yours. This is a forgotten element of using ethereum," he said as the energy began harshly rattling her teeth. It scared her to think they might fly loose from her gums. "Only the Justicars nowadays practice this. Have you ever met one?" he asked as she tightened her grip and clenched her teeth.

Nova thought of her past and recalled one with hair so elegant she would have given anything to touch it. "Yes… she was the most radiant woman I'd ever seen! The prettiest white and gold hair went past her rear." A grin curled across her lips, knowing she could give him an answer as she focused on the blade. What first was the world around her, flooding her body with magic, now felt as if it were drawing from her.

"You've met Lux'ira? That is good. I would like you to think about her. Recall her and use the magic of the node to locate her."

Ajax pulled his hand away from hers. "Keep your hand on the blade until I say so. You need to learn how to communicate across the ley lines." His words came firm enough that she refused to release the dagger until he allowed her to.

With a resolute nod, she shut her eyes and chanted a mantra in the forgotten language of her ancestral court. Something her mother taught her, yet she only knew the words, their meaning lost upon her.

She racked her mind to recall *Lux'ira*. The first thing she remembered was her elegant golden white hair. The second was the divine glow in her wake, and the third was her face that was of such beauty that even the princesses of the Courts envied it in their whispers.

She could feel the node pulling at her, as if seeking to take her beyond her own body. Not permitting herself to hesitate, she allowed the forces pulling on her to yank her soul free from its body, dragging her at breakneck speed through the ley lines. Firing from one node to the next, stopping at intersections before adjusting course, until she came to a stop. Clearly seeing Lux'ira, her heavenly allure did not differ from the first time she saw her over three hundred years prior.

"Good day visitor, to what do I owe this pleasure, my dear? I won't harm you." The words of the female came as tender as her own mothers, yet her mouth hadn't moved. The sound came from within her own mind.

"Oh... hello." Nova's reply was a soft whisper, momentarily shocked, before she focused on talking to the fae

in front of her. *"I'm Nova'ivar. I was told to greet you as part of my training."*

"Job well done! Who is your mentor?" Lux'ira questioned as she sipped at the tea in her hand. The pungent, fruity aroma tickled her nose.

"Ajax," Nova said, as she noted the weightless feeling shrouding her.

"Ah, follow his lessons. He is a wonderful teacher. Every fae he has taught became masters of their craft. Give him a kiss on the cheek for me and tell him he is due for tea. Return to him now. I sadly cannot spend more time with you, Nova. May our fate cross again!" Lux'ira spoke hurriedly before slurping her tea up quickly, her other hand curled in an elegant motion through the air, a golden shimmer appearing at her fingertips.

Beyond Nova's control, she shot through the ley lines again into her body with a sharp intake of breath as she fell back, feeling paralyzed. Upon finding her breath and a few wiggles of her toes to ensure they still worked, she sat up, a hand to her chest. "I met her… and spoke to her," she explained as she pushed to her feet and gave Ajax a kiss on the cheek. "She said to do that and tell you to see her for tea."

With a shake of his head, before a brief chuckle of amusement, Ajax said, "Of course she did. I have sworn to her a tea party for centuries, and I still haven't fulfilled my debt." His tone drifted out so casually, discussing the passing of her entire life as if it were days to him. "How do you feel?"

Nova took in a deep breath as she pondered his question, finding something alive within her that hadn't been there before. "Like my blood is singing..." She spoke in a low whisper as she was disturbingly aware of the world around her, and the magic blooming from everything. She could plainly see Ajax's aura, as well as the distant auras of Shanti, Alana, and Valen.

It was now clear to her that Shanti was a lycan from her earthy aura of greens and browns, while Alana's vampiric aura beat with a constant crimson hunger that flowed from her, something she recognized in herself too. Bright divine flames shrouded Valen which allowed her to feel his warmth even from afar.

The one that had her confused, however, was Ajax. It was clearly ethereal, but beyond fae. She couldn't interpret his aura, which frustrated her. His true nature was incomprehensible, and now she understood why the Seelie King submitted to his presence. Ajax's hand came to her cheek as his eyes focused on hers.

"You were gone for several hours. It is nighttime now. Free your blade. I would like you to use it." His order came in a gentle tone. Had every myth about him been a lie?

After dusting herself off, Nova yanked her blade free from the ground. Every imaginable color pulsed from it, and the power now at her fingertips made her feel as if she could take on the Seelie King on her own. "Do not let temporary feelings from the mana of the Ether sway you. It's a tempting sensation, which is why this is a forgotten tradition. Tapped into improperly and the rush can drive you mad," Ajax said, the warning enough for her second guess following his instruction without a single question.

Ignoring her fear as she took Ajax's words to heart, she held the blade at her stomach, the spine of it pressing into the fabric of her tunic, as her mother's mantra fell from her lips again. His hand came to the small of her back as the other pointed to one of the large fungi. "Cut through the air, and as you feel the mana gather at the tip of your blade, you free it. It will go where you point it." His instructions came in a gentle whisper before he stepped away.

Nova held the blade out and slashed through the air. When she felt no immediate difference; she frowned and tried once more, to no avail. Nova tightened her grip to the point her knuckles turned pale, and slowly pulled a breath in through her nose until she'd filled her lungs, emptying them between pursed lip in a controls push.

Then, she swiped the blade through the air once more, and she felt the energy within the blade slosh, much like a half-filled waterskin. Now she imagined uncorking it as she slashed through the air again, and the vibrant aura within her dagger shot out, slamming into the fungus Ajax had directed her toward. When its top half of the trunk and cap fell to the ground with a clean diagonal slice through it, she jumped up and down cheering. "I did it!"

"Very good Nova," said Ajax, as he began leading her toward the warm ethereal green and red glow of a fire. She could hear Shanti and Alana going back and forth. Over what? She couldn't say.

I can't believe I am learning new magic, she mused to herself as she bounced with each step, feeling content in her progress.

"Do you know what that mantra you say is? Those are powerful ancient words," he said, his sharp gaze drawing her in.

Nova looked at him and shook her head. "Only my mother told me that it's something our people used to say to Buwan," she said, feeling confused by his question.

"Ah, that's close. It's a prayer for Buwan's guidance and wisdom. There is a part for each of the Moons. Would you like to learn the full prayer later?" Ajax asked, as he stopped and she matched him.

Something about having Ajax teach her the words of her people warmed her heart, and she gave him a nod. "Yes, please!" she said with her widest grin.

Ajax's hand came to pat the top of her head. "Pay close attention. I will only teach this once." With a snap of his fingers, the soil beneath their feet changed from orange hued dirt to a flat mound of stone. He settled with his legs under him and an open hand on each knee, and said, "Take my hands."

Nova sat across from him, her knees against his, their fingers intertwined, and she let out a slow inhale and shut her eyes, honing her focus. "I'm ready."

"Open your eyes and look at Buwan," Ajax instructed, his tone hushed to just above a whisper. A tingle of warning shot up her spine as she complied, turning her gaze up to Buwan. This felt more intimate than she could picture someone like Ajax being. Was their skin touching? Ajax's violet magic and her own silvery blue mana mingled together as Ajax began the prayer. "Buwan, may your wisdom guide me even when I am beyond the touch of your gentle light."

CHAPTER 10

THE THREE MOONS

Nova settled beside Valen as he speared his dagger into the belly of a three horned beast. At first, she recoiled as he cut away the meat, only to lean in and watch each movement of the blade. With her hand outstretched while speaking, her repulsion shifted to curiosity. "Can you show me?"

Valen silently taught her to let the blade do the work, and once they'd butchered the entire beast, he stood up and shifted his form, taking that of the elegant bird wreathed in flames he'd shown her. Then, gripping the organs of the beast in his talons, he flew them off into the Feywilds.

As he did so, Nova lifted the platter of mostly well butchered meats, and carried them to the sizable fire Shanti had built using the wood from the tree felled by Ajax. "Just in time! I'm starving!

"Fae beasts are great over an open fire," said Shanti, skewering the meats and placing them on the supports around the fire.

"Have you had this one?" Nova sat beside Alana, leaning against the vampiress; content that even if the journey held danger, she truly was living her dreams.

"Aye, Valen makes a mighty broth with tha' bones, lass. Ye learn yer magic well?" With a wide grin, the vampiress pulled Nova in close, throwing her arm over her shoulder. *Did I?* Nova mused to herself as she rested her head against Alana.

She pulled her blade free from its holster and shrugged. "I learned how to talk over ley lines and dagger magic. Is that good?" She turned a smile at Alana, pride leaving her face aching for having learned so much on her first day.

"A skill that takes most years. Do not fret Nova, you will be plenty capable by our third day. Afterwards, spend a day learning how to fight and another resting," Ajax spoke from behind Alana and herself, his robes different from what he wore prior. These appeared plainer in design, yet she imagined it would feel like being wrapped up in a velvety cloud.

Valen landed a short distance away from their encampment, and after releasing his phoenix form with the plume of flames shrouding him, he strolled over with the bones of the beast in hand. Shanti pointed to the smaller second fire, where a large stock pot sat with water already boiling away.

Nova focused on him, seeing him content to be away from the party, and she pushed herself to her feet and went beside him, pressing her weight into him as he lowered the bones into the water. "I'm still a little scared Valen… were you ever scared like this?" She stepped closer to him and pushed up on her toes to look into the pot.

Valen turned his amber eyes on her and gave her a nod. "Fear never leaves. Only learn to embrace it." His hand came against her back, the warm touch soothing her. Bringing a smile up to the surface of her.

Nova found herself only more confused by his words, blinking rapidly as she sought their meaning. "Can you show me how?" she asked, hopeful he would have wisdom to share.

Her heart sank when his response was a shake of his head. "Lesson, only Nova teach self," he said as he patted her head with a feather-light touch.

Nova puffed her cheeks out in frustration, only more perplexed, and laid out on the ground and shut her eyes, stuffing her worrying thoughts away. She pushed herself up and pointed to the Moons. "Do you know the names of the Moons?"

Valen shook his head as he stirred the broth and skimming scum off the top. She pointed to the first Moon, the one with a faint silvery blue tint to its surface. "That's *Buwan*! My mother was the Grand Priestess of *Buwan*. She told me as a child that she was the guiding light, and the voice of wisdom." When she paused, he gave her a gruff smile that sent warmth spearing through her heart. She adored how intently he listened to her.

"That one is Galach, the ferocious one. The fury and wrath that birthed dragons and malice," she said, now with more gumption as her hands flew emphatically through the air. She finished up by pointing to the vibrantly violet waning sliver of a Moon.

"Third Moon?" Valen asked, pointing to the last one, her color dark crimson with a heart-like beat to her aura.

"Tungl! Mother told me that Tungl is in the hearts of all. She was the first to love, and upon experiencing love, she blessed all to find it in their lives." Nova settled her hands on her lap, finding herself grateful for how he offered her his ear so contently.

The air fell still in the silence between them, and peace and comfort lived in it, one that she knew she would miss.

"Have you ever found love, Valen?" Nova pondered aloud, and he gave a nod.

"Yes. Love many. Ajax, Shanti, Alana, Nova too." He gave her his arm, gently wrapping it around her as she pressed deeper into his side, her face reddened.

"Have you ever mated?" The way he turned his gaze away spoke enough to his experiences.

"Well, you will one day! I know it and she'll be perfect for you. I can't wait to meet her when that day comes." She tried to perk him up and encourage a positive outlook on the future as he'd done for her, and he flashed his gruff grin again and spoke.

"When Fate thinks time is right. Nova want mate?" he asked as he looked to be fixated on Tungl.

His question left her pondering, and she gave him a shrug. "I'd like a mate one day. I don't think I'm ready for one, though," she admitted while rubbing her head. "I hardly know who I am."

"Nova wise," Valen's gentle reply came as he stood up and stirred the broth before gesturing for them to be with the rest of the party. She could hear Alana gleefully singing in her odd language as Ajax and Shanti stared into the flames. Hand in hand with Valen, they came to the group and sat across from Shanti.

"Hey Alana, what are you singing?" Nova asked while idly playing with Valen's large fingers.

"Drinkin' songs, lass! Wha' else are ye supposed ta sing?" Alana said before plopping beside Shanti, only to be shoved backwards off the log. "Now tha' was rude!" Alana let out a groan as she squirmed and sat upright once more. "Ye 'ave any songs ta sing?" she asked before taking a sip from her waterskin.

"Enough singing! The fire is a place for stories as well. Do you know any good ones, Nova?" Shanti cut Alana off as she pulled a cut of meat from the fire and bit into it.

Nova idly spun the ring on her finger and contemplated stories before sighing in dismay. "No, I don't remember the ones told to me in my youth, at least not well enough to tell them," she said, looking away from the group shamefully.

"Well, what good are ya, then? How about you, Ajax? Any good bonfire stories, you knife eared bastard?" Shanti asked as she sent a stick soaring past Ajax's head.

"What of the one about the petulant lycan, whom, in her disrespectful demeanor, found herself as dinner to a fearsome and devilishly handsome fae?" Ajax asked, a faint threat dancing in his tone, and Shanti sputtered in disbelief.

"As if! Fae folk are soft. Only way they're killing a proud and powerful lycan is with underhanded, dishonorable means. Anything better?" Shanti said as she hooted out in an uproar of laugher.

Ajax's gaze fell upon Nova as he replied, "If none of our stories satisfy you, Shanti, perhaps you would be the one to spin a tale for us. Don't you agree, Nova?" he said, startling a reply out of her before she could even think.

"Ah… yeah, you're right Ajax!" she said before she hid herself against Valen's side when the realization she was getting between Ajax and Shanti struck her.

"Fine, side with the smug fucker! I'll remember that when something's trying to eat you!" Shanti grumbled out as she stood up and went over the fire. "Picture a young female, still a pup in the eyes of her Pack, expected to prove herself before her first shift." Shanti spun her tale, and Nova listened intently, finding herself afraid as the girl was sent into a forest filled with dangers beyond her capabilities. The tale took on a darker tone with the girl struggling through the night, injured from a scuffle with a bear, and finding shelter in a small cave as rain poured with the might of gods. When the tale ended with the girl's triumphant battle against a white furred bear, Nova couldn't help but cheer, happy to know she survived her trial. "Still said that to this day, lycan girls idolize her even though time has buried her name in its endless tide."

"That was a fine tale, Shanti. Do you have others of this

heroic lycan female?" Ajax asked, sipping from an elegant crystal glass with a dense brown liquid sloshing about faintly.

"Maybe, but those are for my party when we embark. Consider yourself lucky to have heard it!" Shanti said with an aggressive snarl as she popped her lips free from the bottle. Nova shook her head at the two of them, realizing that they just had a tendency to bicker.

"I've always had dreams of going on an adventure like this." Nova lifted a stick and began drawing the letters, spelling out her own name in the dirt.

"Oi, aye, lass? Ye had dreams of bein' tha' type ta stumble into spooky places haunted by tha' turmoil and wails o' the dead?" Alana asked, her tone dreadful.

Nova scowled, afraid of Alana's gloomy demeanor, and she ran her thumb against her mother's ring, the sensation of the warm metal soothing her. "Yes!" she shouted, biting back her fear, not wanting to be taunted by Alana. "There are so many lost stories in those places… everyone has a story to tell!" she said as she held the highest hope for the best outcomes, despite the impending dangers.

Alana cackled before taking a pull from her bottle. "Atta' lass! Showin' spine! Catch!" She tossed one of her bottles through the flames, Nova flinched and fell backwards, yelping in terror.

The only thing stopping her from a face full of dirt was Valen's hand catching her by the shoulder and bringing her back to sitting upright. Alana's bottle was in his other hand, and he leveled a shrewdly furious glare at Alana, causing her to stick her hands out defensively. "Oi! 'M sorry lass! Won't be taunting ye anymore. Aye?" she spoke out in an apologetic tone.

Nova took a moment to catch her breath, grateful Valen's wrath wasn't directed toward her. "Yeah…" she grumbled out nervously as she slipped the bottle from Valen's hand. "Thank you Valen." She patted his chest before leaning into him. "How do I open this?" She looked back and forth at the group, as Alana pulled another bottle out and opened her mouth.

"Ye've got fangs, lass! Jus' like this!" Alana exclaimed with glee, before sinking one of her fangs into the cork, with a twist of the bottle and a yank. *Pop!* The cork came free of the bottle and Alana flashed a wild grin masked by the cork in her fang. "Ta-da!"

Mortification struck Nova's gut at the idea of using her fangs in such a reckless way, her hand nervously shooting to cover her mouth. "That sounds horrific! My fangs ache just watching that!" she said, muffled through her fingers.

"Help?" Valen asked with his hand out. She handed him the bottle and watched as he pulled out what looked like a piece of dark blue antler from his vest, and used it to remove the cork. He then tucked both back into his vest as he handed Nova the bottle.

"Or ye can do that," Alana pondered with a hand on her chin.

"Get used to watching Alana being the largest ass. Even the Celtic and Nordic gods think she has a problem." Shanti snatched a piece of meat from the fire with a low grumble. "It's ready. Eat."

Nova looked up at Valen, and she gave him a smile. "Thank you again, Valen." Her cheeks reddened when he held out a piece of cooked meat on a stick.

"Need food. Keep strong for journey," Valen's soft words came alongside a gentle pat to the shoulder.

She gave him a nod before leaning forward and biting a chunk off the large cut of meat, setting the bottle down and taking the stick from Valen. The savory, meaty flavor burst across her tongue. "Are all the beasts in the Feywilds this delicious?"

"No. There's plenty of things that taste like soiled loin clothes and rubbish gravy, though!" Shanti replied as she finished her piece and went for another.

"Aye, green fur means it tastes like farts!" Alana sipped to end her statement and Nova's face contorted in disgust at the idea of dining on ass or foot flavored beast.

Next, she focused on eating her dinner, happy to fill her belly, and after a second stick of meat, with a near full belly, she took a sip from the bottle. Sweet and sour flavors bloomed along her pallet, finished with a smoked honey taste at the back of her tongue. "Oh Alana… is this your usual brew?" she asked, holding the bottle toward the sky and catching moonlight on the liquid.

"Aye, ye 'ad it mixed with juice. Neat brew's a mystical experience," Alana said as Nova took another sip, an encouraging dizziness overcoming her. If it weren't for Valen's warmth, she'd be running off to try using her magic in the node.

"Did you bring a lot of it?" Nova slurred out her next

question as she climbed into Valen's lap, cradling the bottle.

"Alana has an endless supply. If her stock runs low, she will bully the witches who make it," Shanti blurted out as she drank from her own bottle. "Don't get used to Valen. He's not coming." She tore apart another chunk of the meat with her teeth, growling at the roughness of the undercooked texture.

Nova looked up at Valen, and her heart sank as she learned that there was no option for him to join them. "Oh…" she mumbled out, curling up against him. She would enjoy the most of it while she had him. "We have a few days… right?" She reached for his hand, not yet ready to part from the giant, who seemed all too content to have her in his lap. His large fingers moved through her hair to untangle it as gently as he could.

Shanti gave a nod, her mouth full of meat. "Yep. Plenty of time to enjoy with everyone's favorite big bastard." From there, the night drifted away into a fog and deep slumber. All she could recall was never losing Valen's warmth.

CHAPTER 11

ARTS OF ENCHANTING

Nova stirred from her sleep, content in Valen's shroud of heat, an unbearable ache tearing through the center of her skull. She whined out against Valen's chest, "My head hurts!" Sniffling as his hand came to rub her shoulder. He pressed his waterskin to her lips and, without a word, she opened her mouth as the cool liquid came rushing to soothe her dry and grimy mouth.

Wrapping her hands around it, she took the waterskin from Valen and gulped away until every drop was gone. "Thank you…" She curled up into the blankets, finding herself drifting back into slumber.

"Stay," Valen said to her before departing from her side, only to return moments later with a bowl of his broth in hand. With his aide, she sat up and sipped at the broth. The first wave that filled her mouth was unimaginably savory, and it cleared the nauseating slosh of her blood from within.

She smiled as she watched him move to refill the bowl for himself. "Thank you, Valen! This broth is amazing. When I finish the journey with Shanti and Alana, can you make me soup again?" She was quick to lean into his warm touch when his hand came against her back, as he tossed back the entire bowl in one gulp.

"My pleasure," he said, with his gruff grin being just what she needed this morning. She was content in pressing her weight against him, sipping broth in silence. She noted that Shanti and Alana were nowhere in sight, while she imagined Ajax took refuge in his cabin.

Two bowls of broth later and Nova stood up, stretching her back out with a low groan. "Fates, I'm getting used to sleeping next to you. Even on the ground, I slept great! I can't wait to learn magic. What'll you do today?" she rambled out all her collected thoughts over their silent breakfast.

"Rest. Fly," Valen said through a yawn, before towering over her by standing up.

"Do you get time to rest often?" she asked as they walked toward the meadow where she'd trained with Ajax the previous day. He gave her a silent nod.

Once they arrived at the meadow, she settled on the mushroom stump and ran her finger over the faint bulge in her palm that covered the compact disc of draconite. She could feel the mana within the stone. Even such a small piece made her feel as if she held the world in her palms. "Do you know any magic, Valen?" She looked at him, studying his face.

"Only fire. Very destructive." His reply came with an undertone of sorrow as his amber eyes turned toward the distant Feywilds.

"Valen's prowess as a phoenix is magical, but the abilities he has are more innate, while magus and fae must train to realize their potential." Ajax's voice came from behind her, his sudden presence sending tension racing across her skin.

Startled, she leaped off the stump and drew her blade without a thought, not even taking the time to process if she was in danger. Ajax stood still, his hands at his sides, in elegant robes just as he'd worn every day. She felt fond of the dark blue and purple shades that made up today's garments. "I admire your gumption, Nova. I don't doubt my verdict. You certainly won't need Valen." He flashed a villainous smirk, as with a faint flick of a finger at her, his dark violet magic sent her dagger flying from her grasp. "We won't be using that today. Leave us Valen. She needs to focus." Without a word, Valen was gone, and now the two of them stood there, a gentle rush of wind blowing by them. "What magic can you do?"

Nova called forth magic to send her rushing toward the tree line and back. "That and little things like how to clean clothes or dishes," she admitted, feeling shameful about how most fae her age had already become skilled in their natural art.

"You have learned what magic feels like and a basic way to

use it, then. That shortens the first lessons," Ajax said as his hand came to her shoulder.

"Over the coming days, we will go over the three schools of practice for an Enchantress, as that is the power you wield," Ajax said to her as he stepped right in front of her, only a foot between them. "The first practice is called *Hugis*." He extended his palm and pure mana pooled, shifting from its colorless mass to matching Ajax's violet aura.

The mystical swirl changed between the forms of various items, ranging from a small vial of ink to a key and several other simple items. "An Enchantress coaxes her mana and the natural energies around her into countless forms. It can extend beyond objects as your skill exceeds the rudimentary." Ajax released the mana, and it took the shape of wings behind his back. Striking lines of varying shades of violet and deep inky black sprawled across the shimmer display.

"Your mother could use the art of *Hugis* to take many forms. Even that of some of the mightiest beasts in the Feywilds. If you have even a fraction of her capabilities, you will find yourself beyond the scant few masters that remain," he said as the wings on his back faded away into a dark violet mist.

Nova listened, her mind blown as her mentor could so effortlessly manipulate the raw mana. Shaking her stupor away, she held out her palms as thoughts of mana flowing in her cupped hands raced through her head. When nothing occurred, her lips contorted in frustration.

"Now, now, Nova, even the best require a helping hand. Ease

yourself. I am going to come behind you and teach you. No one takes their first steps alone." As he'd warned her, Ajax stepped behind her, wrapping his arms around hers and taking her hands in his own.

She noted the silky-smooth texture of his skin, yet he was cold to the touch, as if his body carried no life within it. "Breathing is crucial. Neither too deep..." He took a slow breath, demonstrating one of the few things she had remembered from her mother's lessons. "Nor too shallow. At just the right tempo. Every location is different. Here the mana and air flow free, but as you recall within the Seelie Court, each pull felt as if you were drowning, right?" His hushed question came as she noted the individual lines across his palms. She gave a nod as her eyes focused on his and her intertwined hands.

She took in a slow, calculated breath before exhaling. Nothing felt different. She threw her hands up with an impatient huff. "I only have two more days with you! How will I ever learn this in time?" she grumbled out, stepping out of his light embrace to sulk toward the stump.

"You will do fine. You must not let emotion cloud your mind or sight." His hand came between the blades of her shoulders. "You are far too tense. Sit, we are going to do an exercise my own mother taught me when I was but a fledgling trying to learn how to snuff and light candles." Each word came with a gentle and calming sound to her ears.

She paused as she stared down at her hands. "I don't want to fail you. I want to have earned my freedom, Ajax," she let out in a whimper as she dropped into the stump.

"Those who master an art within their first lessons are short-lived and forgotten," Ajax said, adjusting her sitting position to having her legs crossed beneath her. He stood in front of her and showed her how he'd clasped his hands together. "Place your hands here." He pointed to the triangular gap her legs created from being crossed. He then stood behind her, one palm between her shoulder blades, the other where her spine and hips met. "Only focus on my breathing. Mimic it. Let the world slip away from you, just as you had when using the ley lines," he commanded her in a manner that left it impossible to deny him.

Nova closed her eyes, surrounding herself with darkness. The sound of birds in the distance caught her ear at the same time as Ajax's controlled breathing. The first attempt to copy his breathing failed, the chirping and flapping of wings disturbing her thoughts. "I hear a bird…" she grumbled out. She could feel the mana at Ajax's fingertips against her back.

"Silence Nova. Pay it no mind. Just as in a battle, you will need to ignore the cries of pain and clangs of crossed blades. You must ignore the bird now." Her brows furrowed at his gentle scolding before she straightened her back out and shut her eyes once more. At first, all she could focus on was the distant chatter of birds. Moment after moment passed, and she gradually honed her attention on Ajax's breathing until it was all she could hear and feel. Soon after, her own breath mimicked his tempo.

Once they breathed in unison, Ajax's magic tingled across the entirety of her back, lasting only moments before he pulled away. "Remove your overalls and shirt, please. I require bare skin." Her next set of instructions came, and with an audible *click, click,* she released both clasps of her overalls and then hurried to strip her shirt off. She shivered when his icy hands came against her skin once more, quickly finding unity with his breathing as before. "Good Nova, give yourself in to the sensations entirely. Do not resist," he uttered so soft, she had forgotten her troubles.

Determined to learn, she felt his magic light her entire body up. She was fully aware of every single nerve and the entire network that spanned her body. The epiphany arose as she understood that, just as the ley lines were the network for the magic of the world around them, her body had its own. The most joyous feelings sprawled across her skin, and she nearly arched her back from the pleasurable sensations, as Ajax's palms maintained her fixed posture.

"Now focus on your hands. Flow our joined mana to them." His inaudible whisper came not from his lips, but within her mind. Tilting her head back to draw in a breath, picturing the mana flowing from Ajax through her to take shape in her hands, a faint glow erupted from her hands. *"You did it Nova, your first act of Hugis."* She felt his palms pull away in a slow drift from her own. Next, there came small orbs of violet mana redressing her as she maintained focus.

Slowly, she opened her eyes, staring down at the glow of iridescently white mana in her palms. A smile cracked across her face as she turned to look at Ajax. In that moment, the mana faded away, receding into her body and dispersing into the Ether. "I almost had it…" Dismay struck her face as she lowered her eyes to the ground, shame tearing a hole in her gut with each passing moment.

"Incorrect Nova, you had it. *Breathe. Focus. Shape.* That is how *Hugis* works. Now it is time for you to do it on your own," he corrected her as his gaze seemed fixated off into the distance. "I am proud of you, Nova. You are doing wonderfully. Do not doubt yourself. It will diminish any stride you make." His words of encouragement had her brimming with confidence.

Many silent hours passed, as Nova went from struggling to give form to a brief flicker of mana in her palm, to a bright melon sized orb she could bounce off her hand. Not wanting to wait for Ajax's next instruction as he had slipped away to his cabin, she took it on herself to attempt shaping the mana, spending a moment stroking and spinning her ring in contemplation before she resolved to copy its shape. On her first attempt, the mana burst out in a blinding light, and on her second, as the shape of the ring formed, it fizzled away twice as fast. By the third she'd manipulated the mana into a deformed ring-like shape. She held the misshapen circle in her palms as Ajax came to her side once more. "Dedication like that will take you far." His words carried promise, alongside the subtle grin taking place between his cheeks.

They spent the rest of the day drilling various techniques, and by the time the sun was setting, she'd learned how to use mana to create simple weapons, healing salves, tools, and even how to turn real objects into mana. Although she seemed limited in only being able to create things the size of her palm, and for tools and weapons they lost their shape if she tried to pass them off.

With the rise of Buwan, Ajax summoned a portal with a snap. "You have progressed wonderfully. Rest well, *Ungadh* is difficult. Most Enchantress' struggle with it," Ajax said as he stepped toward the portal.

"When do I learn how to do that?" Nova asked as she tidied the grass stains on her clothes with her silvery blue glowing palm.

"You don't. Realm walking isn't a skill one learns, it is a poisoned chalice Fate forces upon you at birth," Ajax said, cutting the conversation short and departing into his portal. With a yawn, Nova headed to the fire where Shanti was rotating a large, multi-horned beast over the flames. The scent of the meat had her belly aching from hunger.

"*Ungadh*, the second practice of enchanting, as you know means anoint," Ajax said as he raised his fist, shrouding it in a dark purple aura, and punching a nearby large mushroom, knocking it over. "You can empower yourself..." He raised a plain dagger and the aura from his fist took over the blade. "Or turn blades brittle..." His other hand came up to flick the dagger, causing it to crumble like ash. "When you use magic to move quicker than you would be capable. It is the basis of *Ungadgh*," Ajax said.

Her head tilted to the side as a question arose in her. "Is it really that simple?"

Ajax let out a laugh and shook his head. "The basics yes. If you have such an excellent grasp of it already, how about you and Alana race?" he asked, causing her to pause in thought before she nodded.

"I'll go get her!" Nova said, jogging off toward Alana's aura, grateful she wasn't far, as she found the vampiress dangling upside down from the limb of a sturdy pink wooded tree nearby.

Alana swung herself off from the branch, landing beside Nova in an elegant flourish. "'Ello lass, ye hidin' from yer studies?" Her rough hand came up to pat Nova's shoulder.

"Come with me!" Nova took Alana's hand and dragged her toward Ajax, the taller female laughed out and remained firmly on the ground after two steps forward. "Fates, calm yer tits, lass! Let's not gimme tha' rag doll experience I don' want. Aye?" Once they'd exchanged a look, Alana jogged beside Nova; the whole way, a cacophony of snickers shared between them

The two of them arrived at Ajax's turned back, and Nova noted his glassy eyes as he stared off into the distance. Alana approached him cautiously. "Are ya broke lad?" she asked as they arrived in front of him.

"I am perfectly fine, merely lost in thought." Ajax's nostalgic tone and the remnant gaze into the past within his amethyst eyes greeted them. With a snap and dazzle of his violet magic, he neatly adjusted his robes to a state of perfection. "Thank you for joining us, Alana. Please race Nova to the tree line and back." He pointed with his nose, Ajax's tone bore little interest in the present moment.

"On three," Ajax said, as Alana faced the trees, standing perfectly still. "One…" Nova drew a deep breath in through her nose, and let it out through pursed lips.

"Two…" She caught the word, and yet she couldn't match the voice, as her focus narrowed on her target. Her next breath drew in a full chest of mana from the surrounding Ether.

"Three!" The last count came before Nova exhaled as she took off. The haphazard thump of her feet against the ground was the only sound she could even hear, a singular tree her visual fixation. As a throb in the soles of her feet arose, she gritted her teeth and evened out her breathing.

The tree grew closer, and yet Alana was nowhere in sight. Nova's heart raced even harder than she did, leaving her to wonder if the organ would burst from her breast. That was until her foot caught a stone that her eyes had not.

Snap! was the last thing she heard and felt before she let out a curdling screech and everything went dark.

Sometime later, her eyes peeled open, and she found herself staring up at Valen sitting beside her. There was a distinct heat on her left leg. As she looked about, she noticed Valen's hands outstretched to her, bright golden and white flames flickering from his palms. The light was so blinding she couldn't see past her hips. "What happened?" she asked, as a hand came to her cheek.

"Ye busted yer leg, lass." Alana's tender smile filled her periphery. That was when Nova realized her head was in the vampiress' lap.

She reached up to rub at her eyes, feeling disoriented. "Can we still go on the adventure and do all of my training?" She was hopeful her foolish injury hadn't ruined their plans.

Alana nodded and pressed the tip of her finger against Nova's nose. "Aye lass, ye 'ave nothin' ta worry about. Tha big fella's got magic 'ands!" A provocative purr rolled out from her, causing Valen's face to redden and his magic to dampen, while Alana's amusement was clear as her nose wrinkled up and she snickered.

"Would you not be a box of rocks for five minutes?" Shanti's growl came as she squatted beside Valen, her hand coming to rest on Nova's shoulder. "I enjoy hearing that you put the goal first. Keep that gumption up, it'll keep ya breathing. Valen'll have you up and ready to go in no time. Just take it easy. Don't take this for granted. Won't have it in the Feywilds. Push yourself as hard as you can now so you know your limits." Shanti slapped Valen's back before stomping off, as Nova tracked the imprints of her boots on the soil.

Once she'd left, Valen turned his gaze toward Nova and nodded. "Limits trick mind play on body." He pulled his hands away from her leg and she looked over the limb.

Not even scars remained. She ran her hand over her shin and smiled at Valen. "Thank you, Valen!" she said, leaning up to hug his side. His pause before meeting her embrace was a constant. She wondered why he seemed so hesitant when approached with affection. *I doubt he'd talk about it. Maybe Shanti or Ajax know?* she mused to herself. She wished to understand him more.

"All better? How feel?" Valen stepped back from her, his

eyes turning toward something distant.

Nova leaped at him for one more hug and she sighed out, "Much, I'm sorry if I disturbed your day." She dropped her eyes to the ground, and she prayed to Buwan that Valen would be forgiving.

"Never disturb. Always happy be useful." For the first time, his voice beamed with pride. She couldn't help but smile at the vibrant glow in his eyes as he swelled up with joy at the idea of providing for others. His hand came against her back as he walked with her toward the meadow.

Without a thought, she reached out for his hand and nodded, opting for silence through the rest of their walk as her mind raced in every direction; from her training to understanding all of her companions better, to what trials she might face along the way.

"See later!" A gentle pat from Valen's massive hand to the top of her head was his final greeting before taking off.

Straight afterwards, Ajax appeared at her side, which had her nearly leaping out of her own skin. "Are you well? That injury is a wonderful transition into reinforcing with *Ungadh*." His tone left her wondering if it were trivial that she split her leg in two.

She gave him a nod of her head and looked at her shin. "I'm ready!" she said, the excitement had her aura pouring out from her hands, as Ajax stepped in front of her and took hold of her wrists, dragging her into a position with her arms raised high above her head. He nudged her feet shoulder width apart with his own foot.

"There, now you're in a better position to practice. As you might tense a muscle, do the same with your energy." Ajax took his own stance and swung his fist gracefully at her arms, breaking the very guard he'd set up for her.

Nova stood there, resetting her guard as Ajax threw his punches at her, her eyes locked on her arms as she strained to focus her mana up to them.

Nova's arms trembled as Ajax's strikes landed upon them, with only a failed attempt to harden herself in preparation. Each blow stung sharply against her skin, as she gritted her teeth, struggling to focus her mana. Just as she began to feel the sensation of the mana tightening up around her arms, Ajax's next hit broke her focus.

"Patience, Nova. Do not force it." Ajax's voice came calm as he spun her around and took her hands.

With a frustrated huff, she locked her gaze with his piercing amethyst eyes. "Is there a different exercise?" She pulled her hands away from his and they immediately felt as if she had stuck her hands into a fire. "Ow! Ajax! Why did you burn me?" she said, blowing air at her hands.

"A different exercise. Take my hands." Ajax's tone came so firm, like a command she found she couldn't disobey. She placed her hands in his once more, and as their skin came together, she felt her mind drawn from her body and forced to fixate entirely on the connection between their palms and his voice. "Pardon the intrusive technique, but I required a similar one when Sela taught me." His voice drifted out with an odd *warmth,* as if there was a coo to each syllable. "It is the only way to truly show you the mana working in action for *Ungadh*."

When he mentioned mana, it drew her focus to the waves of energy flowing around her, Ajax's deep violet hues flowing seamlessly with her silvery blues. That was until his coalesced and shrunk inward, tightening from unbound waves into a wall denser than stone. Without form, Nova floated in an endless expanse of shimmering color.

She felt Ajax's presence nearby, their energies mingling. When she tried to touch his violet mana, only to find she had neither hands nor fingers, only tendrils of light bearing the hues of silver and blue of her own inner power controlled purely by thought Nova watched in fascination as her mana splashed harmlessly against Ajax's impenetrable wall. Though she had no physical form, her frustration was palpable.

"Don't force," Ajax's gentle reminder came. "Observe."

Nova focused on the violet mana, studying how Ajax shaped it with such ease. Meanwhile, her own swirled with unbridled chaos, refusing her attempts to direct it. She drew in a slow breath, reminding herself of Ajax's breathwork, and with each passing exhale, the tides of her mana settled on a glassy surface.

With a thought of prodding the wall, a single tendril of her mana shot out from the mass and came against the stoney exterior. Her mentor's essence felt rigid, like the tightest string of a harp on the verge of snapping.

"Allow your mind and body to adjust." Ajax's guidance came as his hand on her back stilled her from swaying. Her stomach churned wildly and her hands flew to wrap around it. "That will pass. Astral projection to that state is quite taxing. Sit and meditate," he commanded her, pointing to the stump. Without a word, she sat in the cross-legged position he taught her.

Nova watched as Ajax began walking toward his cabin, then she shut her eyes and directed her attention to thinking about what had just happened. *Why is he making me meditate? We should do magic until I pass out*, she grumbled in her mind. Nova wrapped her hands around her knees and drew in a slow and deep breath until her lungs felt as if they might burst, then she held it until she sputtered out in a fit of coughs.

"That's not meditation, silly." A distinctly familiar whisper drifted from every direction in her mind. She shut her eyes as tight as she could, ignoring the voices of an ather deprived mind.

A hand came to cradle her chin, and as she opened her eyes, Nova realized she was no longer near the Feywilds. The vibrant and expertly curated northern garden of the Seelie Palace surrounded her. Off to her left, she could hear the gentle flow of water from the stone fountain, chiseled to depict an ancient Seelie Warrior who fought alongside a dragon god.

"Over here Nova'ivar!" The most tender scolding sounded out as a hand on her chin forced her to look up into elegantly long unbound blue hair much like her own, and eyes that matched her own, yet the skin was pale as a Moon. The female who held her chin dipped down to kiss her forehead.

With no control of her own, Nova's body erupted in squeals. "Mama! You slobbered all over my forehead," her compact form shrieked out, as her body moved to wipe the remnants of her mother's kiss.

"Focus my savage little magpie!" Sela'mann cooed out as she released Nova's chin, all the while blowing a kiss at her. "You'll need this one day, I promise." The tender words came as a dagger to the heart, as Nova's mind raced with so many unanswered questions. There was so much she had to learn, and more than any burning curiosity, Nova craved to understand her lost past.

The world changed in the blink of an eye, the meadows rushing back to her as the northern gardens faded away. Just as quickly as it had offered her a moment to commune with her mother, it was gone. Into the emptiness. Her hand stretched out, heart tightened into a knot in her chest as she sighed, her eyes dropping to her ring as she spun it over her finger. She found that with several days of a full stomach, the ring was slightly tighter now, and while she could still sway it, it held noticeable resistance.

After many long moments of stilling her thoughts and spinning her ring, she found her mind grew silent, and she tucked herself back into the cross-legged position both her mother and Ajax preferred. Next, came hooking her thumbs along the sides of her head to tuck her hair behind her ears, as she shut her eyes once more and steadied her breathing to an even tempo.

"Slip away from the realm of flesh. Flesh is deceptive." Sela'maan's tender voice rang through her skull.

With a controlled exhale, she imagined herself back where

Ajax had her, caught in the energetic tides of mana that she yearned to wield with expertise. She soon found herself wrapped up in a soothing aura, her own silvery blues swirling about her. What should have been an ocean drowning her, simply felt as natural as breathing. She drew the wisps into her lungs as she imagined the sea turning to stone, her mana coalescing around her, encircling her in a solidified half dome.

She reached her hand out to touch it and, unlike the dome of Atlantis, this one was solid, yet when she pounded her fist against it, the barrier was sturdier than stone. Her hand now splayed out against it as she thought of it passing through. What only minutes ago seemed impossible now came with a simple motion of the mind.

She practiced dropping and reshaping the barrier multiple times, as the idea of making a smaller barrier to deploy faster struck her. She began focusing on creating smaller shields just larger than her palms, finding that they deployed with minimal effort and in the blink of an eye.

She jumped to her feet and ran toward Ajax's aura, shouting out his name, only to be startled by his appearance behind her. "You do not need to bellow for me. I would have come to a soft beckon," he said as they walked back to the meadow.

"I'm ready!" Nova said as she held up her hands, flashing barriers of hardened light at her palms. When Ajax took a swing at one of them, only to reel back, shaking his hand in the air.

A grin crossed his sharp ethereal features, and his hand clapped lightly on her shoulder. "Good, that is all for today. You have certainly exceeded my expectations. Sela'maan would be quite proud of you," he said in a tone that was eerily tender for Ajax, as he led her toward a hunched over Valen, who lit the fire with a breath of colorful flames bearing a range of blues to reds and bright white tips.

⚜

Nova tossed beside Valen. She'd managed a scant two hours of rest. Her mind raced with wonder, rendering returning to sleep impossible. Ajax's glimpse into the next batch of lessons fascinated her beyond belief. She sat up and pushed to her feet. The Moons hung high as she snuck off from the campsite back to the meadow, taking the time to recall the phases of the Moons and their meanings. Buwan stood in her fullest glory, yet Tungl and Galach held opposing waning and waxing slivers.

The meadow stood serenely bathed in Buwan's pale, silvery light, as Nova hurried toward it before settling down atop the stump. She stared upward at Buwan, tracing the erratic pattern of blue speckles across the otherwise pristine surface with the tip of her finger, leaving a trail of her magic across the spots until a senseless shape of connected lines formed. "Do you beckon me back to the meadow, Goddess Buwan?" she whispered out to the Ether, certain that despite her mother's service to the goddess, she had greater things to focus upon than a lost and courtless former slave.

With a slow inhale, she shut her eyes, letting the sounds of the night flood her mind. An insect's chirping in the distance, accompanied by a gentle gust toward her companions, was all she heard. She crisscrossed her legs and flattened her palms against the surface of the stump's smooth and firm texture, moving her hands toward the center in search of a connection to life. Surely, even though it was dead, what remained would be connecting her to the land itself.

She found the faintest flicker, barely even a spark, and she formed her index fingers and thumbs into a triangle around it and fixated on it, only to be fallen with dismay when her own mana gorged the last bit of life within the now quickly decaying stump.

She leaped off it as it crumbled to ash, her lips curled to a frown as she dropped to her knees at the now dark gray pile of what remained. She splayed her palms out toward it, burying them into the dry mass.

With each breath, she envisioned feeding life back into the mushroom, returning it to its former glory. A burst of light had caught her by surprise before she soared through the air, colliding into the ground several strides away.

Now rubbing at her eyes as she sat up, finding herself exhausted once more, Nova yawned. Every single bone ached. She settled her hands in her lap with a huff until she caught sight of the result of her tinkering about with magic.

The ashen pile now stood as the tallest mushroom in sight, triple the size of the others. So massive it even would have Valen appearing small. It had a faintly glowing mane that matched her own aura. It *breathed* with life that was her own and yet not. Curiosity racked her mind as she got to her feet and rushed to the stalk.

She leaned her back against the exposed trunk and slid down to sit on the ground. In moments, sleep overtook her.

She woke to the sun stinging her shut eyes, Shanti and Alana arguing about something in the distance. She was uncertain and cared little for their squabbles, as she raised a hand to shield her eyes while prying them open with a yawn.

"Good morning, Nova, I see you stayed up late practicing your Hugis. Breathing life is not a simple talent. You bear your mother's gifts beyond her beauty." Ajax's voice caught her ear as the first thing that filled her eyes wasn't the sun or her mentor, but Valen sitting in front of her with a cup in his lap.

The massive male gave her a hidden smile as he held the cup with its delightful aromas before her, and she gently wrapped her hands around it and took a sip. "Good morning, Ajax and Valen, thank you," she let out in a soft, husky mumble.

The morning passed rather silently, the three of them enjoying tea as Alana and Shanti's disputes drifted further and further away. Nova even happily held Valen's hand by the time she finished her tea.

With a snap from Ajax, the cup vanished from her palm. "It is time to begin. Miryoku is learning how to bend the wisps of emotional energy to your whims. Few ever learn the true depths, only resorting to use it for simple beguilements and illusion," he said in a hushed tone.

"Before we start, can I ask both of you a question?" Nova asked as she shifted back so she could see both males.

"Why, of course, Nova. What is on your mind?" Ajax's reply came as he leaned back to find a more relaxed position.

Nova scratched the side of her head in thought for a moment to ensure she had the right words. "How do I know when I'm truly living life to the fullest?" she inquired in a low voice, ashamed to ask such a thing.

Ajax let out a brief chuckle. "That is simple. You learn to live like that when you come to understand the gravest truth of life: in the end, no one is coming to save you. You are at the whims of your own choices. You have been saved once. It is more than most ever get," he said coldly, yet his words stuck in her mind.

In the end, no one is coming save you. She found a place for the continued echo of his words in her mind near Shanti's mantra. *Survive, adapt, thrive*, she mused. She felt so utterly ridiculous for finding power in just a few words from mighty individuals. As the thought consumed her, Ajax snapped in front of her eyes to draw her attention.

"Fates! My apologies. Thank you, Ajax," Nova said, as she banished the fog from her mind and set her hand on Valen's. Just as he was always quick to reassure her, she wanted to offer him the same comfort, even if he didn't need it. She was certain he had an answer of his own which she would seek later.

Ajax shook his head and patted his hand gently against her shoulder. "Gather yourself. I'd like you to focus on Valen," he instructed, as he moved to stand behind her. With a deep breath, she set her eyes on the massive male and drew her hands to her lap.

Breathe steady, she reminded herself as she filled her lungs with a deep pull through her nose, stretching her chest out as far it might extend before pushing a wisp of controlled gust through pursed lips. A rich aura that matched Valen's eyes shrouded him, so warm that, as always, just seeing him made her crave to hide away from the world in his lap. Shaking her head to send those thoughts away, she now fixated on the handle of his great sword. It was so simple. She wondered why, if he had access to all the same fineries as Ajax, he still presented himself so plainly. Was that the thing she loved about him so much? His sheer lack of care for the vain efforts her kin fussed over endlessly, be they Seelie or Unseelie.

"What is he feeling now?" Ajax's words came as a faint beckon in the distance, and yet it was enough to pull her away from the maze of her racing mind.

As she stared upon Valen, studying not him specifically, but the shroud of amber hues billowing about him, not with the wind but by his own beating heart. Something she could faintly sense as she recalled the flavor of his blood across her tongue. A dangerously delightful meal... even if she loathed the act of feeding, doing it with Valen, she felt safe and unjudged. "Nova! You keep letting your mind conquer you. Stop allowing your thoughts to wander," Ajax scolded her calmly, his fingers pressed into her shoulder, snapping her back to reality.

With a jolt, she looked about nervously, before falling silently back into her focused mindset, this time shoving any thoughts involving herself away, cramming them into the depths of her mind as she drew in a deep breath. Valen's aura felt so palpable with every inhale, the Ether replaced little by little with wisps of *him*, until her very lungs felt encased in his warmth.

As Nova shoved her own sensations of life away, she felt herself slipping into his essence, immersed in the warm amber hues. At first, there was only comfort and reassurance, like basking in the glow of a hearth fire.

A crushing weight settled on her shoulders, so heavy it made her gasp. She sensed a yawning abyss tucked away in Valen's spirit, something ancient and unspoken that gnawed away at the male.

It was a bone-deep feeling of unworthiness, that no matter how tender and selfless his actions, Valen believed he was wholly unworthy. This inner void drove him to push himself far past exhaustion, to take on any burden, because even if he felt undeserving of affection, his life could still be of use. *Be light for others.* An errant thought, foreign from her own, streaked across her mind in the male's husky tones.

Nova's breath hitched at this glimpse into Valen's inner turmoil. She longed to embrace him and insist she valued him just for being himself. Yet she felt her own pit… an understanding that she would never have the word or touch to be the salve to his heart. She loathed that fate had been anything less than the kindest to him. *Why him?* was the first thought of her own to surface. She found her cheeks had become stained with tears, and Ajax had his hand rubbing gently against her back.

Tears welled up in her eyes once more, then the full weight of Valen's unspoken anguish settled upon her. He bore this immense, secret pain, all while comforting and supporting everyone around him. Nova's shoulders shook with barely contained sobs. She wanted nothing more than to take all the darkness from him, though she knew it was not her place. Still, she vowed to herself that she would be whatever source of light she could, for however long fate allowed her to remain by his side.

"Center yourself. Valen and I shall give you space, so you do not have our emotional matrixes interfering with your own," her mentor stated before she found herself alone. She stuffed her worry for Valen away, even though she knew of his pain and wished to soothe it. She had her own wounds to heal and battles to face.

Nova sat there in the empty meadow, struggling to temper the turbulent winds of her own emotions after the brief glimpse into Valen's inner turmoil. As much as every fiber of her being yearned to embrace him and be the light that relieved his pain, she knew it would never be. It left her heart so raw that although he was her savior, she could only offer him brief comfort. In days she'd admired him so greatly, she found herself determined to make everyone around her proud of her, proud they rescued a once worthless slave.

Soft footfalls soon approached, and her mentor emerged to stand before her. "Have you centered yourself?" Ajax inquired, to which she replied with a simple nod.

"Then let us resume your lesson," he declared as he extended his hand out toward her. She took it without hesitation, allowing him to guide her back to her feet. "Emotions hold great power, as you've witnessed. With time and practice, you will learn the value of control over them."

Nova listened intently as Ajax held a hand out, taking hers in his. A sense of peace and calm consumed her entirely. The anxieties that churned within fell away so quickly, replaced only by tranquil stillness. It was as though the entire world had faded away, leaving only this moment of serenity. She wondered if she could ever attain this state on her own.

"Now, return the favor. Make me feel... amused," Ajax then instructed, dropping the spell that shrouded over Nova's mind. She stared at him for a few silent moments, uncertain if she could truly wield such energies; the experience with Valen's still leaving an ache swirling in her chest. The sharp glint in his vibrant amethyst eyes encouraged her even when she questioned herself.

Taking a deep breath, Nova extended her senses toward Ajax, seeking the strands of his emotional matrix. But she quickly found her own roiling feelings kept diverting her focus, making it impossible to isolate his essence. The more she strained and grasped, the more the emotions slipped through her fingers.

Frustration mounted as her attempts failed again and again. Nova knew she was capable of this, if only she could find peace. Ajax had unlocked something within her during their very first lesson, and she would be damned if she let it all slip away now.

With teeth clenched so forcefully her jaw ached, Nova forged ahead recklessly. Losing a fierce cry, she sent jagged tendrils of energy lashing violently toward Ajax's mind, his face contorting as the emotions she forced upon him clearly caused great distress.

"Control, Nova," Ajax urged, his voice tight. "You must find balance."

But Nova had no intention of stopping now. She had come too far to turn back. She doubled her efforts, imposing her will with brute magical force. Crimson blood dripped from Ajax's nose, yet still Nova did not relent. She would master this magic tonight, no matter the cost.

"Stop. You must not use this power until you have found peace within. It will destroy weaker minds," Ajax said as he raised his hand to pinch his nose. A soft glow appeared at the tips of his fingers. In moments, the blood flow ceased, and it rendered any stains non-existent. "I believe this is where we shall end for today. Do not use Miryoku until I can train you more deeply. Only focus on reading others. That in it of itself can prove to be such a powerful tool."

Nova frowned while lowering her head in defeat. She felt terribly guilty for having inflicted pain on one of her liberators, a male who, despite the fearsome tales behind him, had shown her nothing but patience and kindness. "Is there anything I can do to make up for the pain I've caused?" she asked, trying to keep her voice steady.

"Oh, it is no great ordeal, Nova. I knew this could very well happen. It does with most of the first few lessons in Miryoku. You have done well for your first time. One day, you shall be even more skilled than Sela. For now, you must rest, as nothing ensures the progress of learning any skill more than staying well rested," he said as he aided her to stand, the two of them now walking toward the campsite.

The crackling fire bathed Alana's features in a warm glow as her voice carried into the night. She sat atop a weathered log, eyes closed, and a hint of a smile on her lips as she sang. Her lilting tones rose and fell with each verse, the words flowing together in a rhythmic chant in a dialect unknown to her. Though she could not comprehend the lyrics, the cadence reminded her of ancient ballads she'd heard palace bards perform. Alana's voice evoked images of misty hills weathered stone, and wispy stalks of flora swaying in the wind. Her melodies danced like a playful stream tumbling over rocks, with bursts of raw emotion cresting through. As the last note faded, Alana's smile grew broader, her soul nourished by the familiar old songs of her people.

"Can you teach me to sing like that?" Nova asked as she sat near Alana.

The vampiress gave a nod and slung her arms around Nova's shoulders. "'Course lass! Anythin' to pass the gift o' song on!" Alana said with the sweetest grin.

The evening drifted away, with Alana teaching Nova to sing a song in fae that she knew, which she found enchantingly charming, despite being horrifically butchered by Alana's fae. They sang, drank, and ate soup and dried meats from the previous hunts.

As the fire died down to glowing embers, Nova's eyelids

grew heavy, and she bid Alana goodnight and curled up in her bedroll, comforted by the vampiress' singing still echoing in her mind, and the cradle of Valen's heat. Tomorrow would bring Shanti's combat lessons, but for now, she let the crackling fire and chirping insects of the night lull her into a peaceful sleep. Her final thoughts were on how she could show Valen appreciation before the end of their time together.

CHAPTER 12

FIGHT LIKE A BITCH

Nova's comfortable spot snuggled up to Valen was suddenly stripped away by a hand on her ankle, dragging her through the grass and dirt. "Get your ass in motion!" Shanti's shout came, right before she haphazardly slung Nova, sending her tumbling across the ground.

Nova sat up, glaring at Shanti, her hair and clothes a mess, her mind still tumbling even if she remained still. That was until the blonde yanked her to her feet. "That was rude…" Nova huffed.

"The sun's rising. You rise with it." A forceful pat stung Nova's back as Shanti spoke. "You need to learn how to fight like a bitch with a clue! Square off," Shanti said, as she fell into a fighting stance, hands balled up into fists tucked defensively close to her chin, feet set firmly apart. Nova studied the form until it was seared into her memory.

She attempted to match the rigid form, only for her legs to be swept out from under her. "Oof…" she grunted out when her ass hit the ground. "You can't fight like that. You need balance. Get back up. That's your first lesson. No matter how hard you fall, you don't stay down unless you're dead. Avoid the ground," Shanti said as she began kicking her sides. At first, her instinct was to curl up and protect herself, shielding her sides with her elbows, but as the impact grew harsher and more pinpointed, the tip of Shanti's boot being driven into her organs, Nova realized she'd never be able to survive like this.

Now determined to escape from the crushing force, she eyed an opening to slip away. As Shanti reared back for another kick, she rolled to the side of the blonde, pushing herself upright. "Always expect to wind up at a disadvantage. Remember the golden rule: survive, adapt, thrive."

Nova fixated on Shanti's creed, as she watched her teacher approach, swinging a kick at her waist. She leaned to dodge, only to catch Shanti's boot on the side of her head. Dazed by the impact, she pushed forward, each step uneasy as she planted her feet on the ground, finding balance, right as Shanti came at her.

The first kick came, and she blocked it with her shin, dodging the second with an evasive side step, as the opportunity to strike caught her eye. She threw her full might at Shanti's ribs, yet knuckles collided against her chin, sending her onto her back once again, staring up at the fearsome blonde above her. She rubbed at her chin before jumping back to her feet quicker than the last time. "Good. Good, you can get up when you're down. Now you need to learn how to not throw a childish punch." Shanti's grin, alongside the sparkle in her green eyes, left Nova concerned that the training would kill her before the journey.

"I did my best…" Nova said, feeling a wave of defeat crash down upon her shoulders, yet the determination to become something greater than a worthless slave burned in her gut. Even if she was unsure what she sought in life, she knew it would lead to her making everyone proud.

"Square off!" Shanti's bark of a tone came, and Nova followed her order without question. The lycaness came to her side and began adjusting the placement of her arms and feet. After a few moments, she was in a rigid stance, and it felt entirely natural to her. "Now, throwing a punch isn't about hitting with your fist like a singular movement. A good strike uses your entire body. Alana! Get over here!" Shanti yelled out.

"Aye? Ye were wailin' fer me?" The brunette vampiress rushed over to them near instantly, and Nova hoped she would be able to move like her one day.

"Punch her," Shanti commanded, while pointing at Alana, and Nova threw her fist at her, striking her in the chest.

"Lass yer gon' need more than a wee baby's punch," Alana's critique came, as Shanti swung a punch that appeared effortless for her, striking Alana in the chest exactly where Nova's hit landed, yet Shanti's sent Alana several feet back onto her ass.

"Watch me," Shanti instructed, as she punched the air with elegant fluid motions. Nova studied the way the blonde's body moved; not just her fists, but following along her arms, to her chest, even down past her core. When Nova realized that, punching went beyond a wild flail of the arm. Shanti's unyielding might came from a refined technique of coordination from the soles of the feet upward.

"Follow." Shanti stopped striking the air and led Nova over to where the tree line of the Feywilds began and pointed at one with her thumb. "Strike until I stop you," she said, seeing no oddity in her words. Nova couldn't fathom why this was an exercise, but Shanti knew better.

Hesitantly, Nova obliged, crying out at the first strike as it split the flesh on her knuckles, yet she focused on the dark purple bark, her copper eyes locked on the splash of red of her own blood. She struck the tree again and again, with Shanti's occasional adjustments. With each hit came a faint deadening to the pain, as her cries turned to grunts, which ceased entirely after near two hours of the exercise.

Shanti grabbed her wrists and pulled Nova's focus to look at her bloody and bashed hands. "Look at your hands. What do you see?" Nova's features contorted into a quizzical glare as she stared at the pale flesh stained red with her own blood.

"My beat-up hands?" she pondered aloud, only to be met with Shanti's hand ruffling her hair.

"Yes, obviously. Look for more than just busted knuckles," Shanti chuckled out with a grin.

Once again focusing on her hands, she noticed faintly exposed bone sticking out, as blood leaked uncontrollably down onto the grass below them. The same pride she felt in learning magic flooded her. "I want to spar," she spoke out quietly, determined to challenge Shanti.

"Soon. We have a few more lessons before you're ready. Clean yourself up. You have five minutes," Shanti said before slapping her back hard enough to send her off the ground.

Nova gave a nod to Shanti and walked off, continuing to focus on her knuckles. She concentrated her thoughts on manipulating her mana to re-knit the flesh and strip blood and flecks of purple bark. At first, she struggled to get the mana flowing, her breathing still labored from her training. So, she stopped moving and shut her eyes, the sound of birds in the distance distracting her.

With a slow inhale, the *chirps* and *tweets* drifted away, and she held the air in her lungs for several seconds before releasing it slowly. Several controlled breaths later, and she could feel the rhythmic beat of the Ether, through the ground at her feet, and mana surrounding her all pieced together into an elegant symphony that was felt across all her senses.

She synchronized her breathing with the harmony of the three, and her eyelids drew open carefully. She was shocked by how her vision had changed entirely. Everything around her carried a faint hue of color around it. The air was a constant flowing river of wispy arctic blue. She spotted Valen in the distance carrying a fresh kill on his shoulder, a warm amber just like his eyes surrounding him. For a moment, she let herself get lost in his heat before returning her focus to her hands, her own aura invisible to her.

Just as each breath filled her lungs with air, it drew mana into every fiber of her body. Her entire body flooded with energy, as a rush from the power at her fingertips buzzed through her. She dropped to her knees, seeking more contact with the ground, with her hands splayed out against the dirt. The wounds across her knuckles returned to their original state, as the blood and grime evaporated off her hands and wrists.

Lost in thought, she found herself disoriented as she was pulled to the ground and dragged through the dirt. "Daylight's burning! We've got a lot to cover!" came Shanti's callous shout, her hand pulling at Nova's collar.

It took a few moments of Nova's entire world feeling askew to shake away the daze shrouding her mind. She pried Shanti's fingers away and pushed to her feet. It was difficult to keep up with the taller female's strides, but she managed jogging alongside the harsh lycaness. "What am I learning?" she asked as they moved into an area that was cleared of grass from one of Valen's landings.

"Defending yourself," Shanti replied as they came to a stop at a large patch of torched soil. Nova stopped two steps away from Shanti.

"How?" she asked as she began scratching at her scalp. She wondered if they would ever find water they could bath in in the Feywilds. Even if she had magic at her fingertips, the idea of enjoying the ethereal waters of the Feywilds against her skin had her lost in thought.

"I'm going to hit you. Either you learn to not get hit or you die," Shanti said as she looked at her own nails, an inaudible sigh leaving her lips before jabbing Nova in the head.

Nova's brow furrowed in confusion. "I didn—" The foot that collided with the side of her head knocked the light from her eyes; one moment she was upright, the next she was laid out on the cool ground, the blue and orange rays of the ever-changing sun of the Ether warming her cheeks as she eyed the green and violet tapestry of the cloud free sky.

"10... 9... 8..." Shanti began counting down from ten as Nova curled up in shock from the throb pulsating between her ears. "Stop counting! My head is killing me!" Nova cried out, yet Shanti continued. "2... 1..." As Shanti stopped making noise, the moment of silence was a taste of the divine, only to be disrupted by Shanti driving her foot into Nova's back. "Get up!" Shanti drove another kick into Nova's side.

"10... 9..." Nova let out a groan as she tried to shift her focus from the pain across her head and back. With a peel of her eyes, the plain copper band cradling her ring finger caught her attention, and she clenched her left hand, fingers covering her thumb as she ran the tip across her mother's ring. "6... 5..." Shanti hummed out as she bounced on her boots. With a controlled breath, Nova pushed herself to rise and quickly find balance. "You learn quick. Stay nimble. Come at me." Shanti's order came as the taller female stood with her fists balled up and feet squared off, prepared to fight.

Nova gave a nod and took a jab at Shanti, who effortlessly stepped away from the punch. Shanti blocked the next strike with her forearm, only to knock Nova's chin with a firm yet restrained thrust of knuckles on bone. Nova stepped back with a recovered stumble, her hand rubbing at her aching chin. "Watch how your opponent moves. Most are predictable. A confident swagger can be deceptive."

She stepped back into the stance imprinted into her mind, throwing a punch at Shanti's chest. Shock came when a harsh grip clenched her wrist and, with a fluid motion, Shanti threw her into the dirt. "Re-direction. Turn an attack even from much larger and stronger foes into planting them like a seed."

Nova rolled herself into a crouch before pushing herself upright, then she leaned in, aiming for a gut shot. Shanti's elegant evasion came with her, weaving to the left and sending an open palm for Nova's cheek. Reflexively, Nova shot her knee upwards, flinching to avoid the impending slap as she felt her knee slam into Shanti's core. Shanti stepped back and laughed, clapping Nova harshly on the back. "You're doing great! You hit me! This is going to be a fun morning!" the tall blonde cheered, her tone equally encouraging and fear inspiring.

⁂

Nova's entire morning was spent learning how to fight by having Shanti throwing every imaginable attack until she could defend herself from it. After training, she rubbed at the muscles in her arms while walking alongside Valen. "Fates… I feel like one of the dragon gods chewed upon me," she said with a desire to sleep scratching at her mind.

"Shanti, excellent teacher. Did well." Valen's compliment came with his arm around her. A gentle rub of his warm hand against her shoulder soothed the ache, as the scent of food cooking teased her nose. Even though it was only meat, she never felt more satisfied. She thought back to how she only ever ate a mushy gruel or mixed leftovers. "Need blood?" Valen's soft question disturbed her, as her mind wandered off in thought.

"I can go long without it… you don't have to if you don't want to Valen," Nova replied, nervously fidgeting with her ring.

The large male shook his head and patted his hand gently against the back of her hair. She could easily find herself lost in the delicate sensation. "Long journey. Feed before. Gave Alana blood," he said so sweetly, she found her teeth aching.

She looked up at him and stepped into wrapping her arms around his core. "Maybe. I'll ask later if I need it, okay?" she asked Valen as they continued their walk to the campsite.

Alana was the one cooking now, a heavy metal frying pan in her hand. "Mornin' lass! Ye 'ave a seat, went and did some foragin' an' found enough to make a right proper *bourie*." Nova looked at the sizzling pan, seeing the meat cooking. The scent had her stomach doing backflips, and mouth pooling with saliva.

"That smells so good, Alana! What else is there?" Nova asked as she watched Valen effortlessly crush hard shelled fruit with his bare hands to bring forth juice. In this moment, she wondered how he could be so mighty, yet gentle. She imagined him being as tender as he was with her never came easily. The way he always seemed to shrink himself around others made sense to her now, he was vividly aware of the great harm he could cause and that fear ruled over him through his daily life. She wondered if there would ever be words that could soothe him.

"Got 'taters goin' in another pan ta' me right. After tha' meat is done, a couple eggs fer each o' us," Alana said with glee, lighting her eyes as Nova's hand came to her grumbling and groaning belly.

"When will we get to eat like this again?" Nova took her gaze off Valen to focus on the vampiress before her, slaving away over a fire and pan.

"Ye've got lotssa questions, lass. Sit yer arse down and just focus on what's in front of ye, aye?" Alana said, as she shook a wooden spatula at her. Without a word she obliged and leaned into Valen, who handed her a cup of juice that was a blend of green and orange hues swirling together yet not mixing. She was happy to take it and press her lips to the cold glass for a sip. A burst of sweetness came first, but it quickly turned into an enjoyable smooth tartness spreading across her palette.

"What did the fruit look like in case I see more of it?" She leaned against Valen, looking up at him as he picked up a fiery yellow and icy blue hard-shelled fruit.

She took it into her hands and ran her fingers across the harshly coarse yet fuzzy exterior, avoiding the spikes sticking out across the upper third of the fruit. "Trollsbane. Ripe only like this. Other colors poisonous," Valen said, as she passed the fruit back to him, which he set aside with the others.

"Are there lots of fruits in the Feywilds?" Her hand found Valen's. Even if it was temporary and she knew it, she wanted as much of the connection as she could get with him. She wanted to show him that even if they had different paths in life, he was more than whatever darkness he saw in himself.

"Oi lass, after grub I'm the one training ye, so ye'd bes' nae be pissin' me off, aye? Relax. Yer nae gon' starve." Alana slapped the hot wooden spatula against her calf and Nova pulled back in a startled shriek.

"Fine! I just like to learn!" she yelped out before moving to the other side of Valen. His hand held out a leather-bound journal.

"Learn to read?" he offered, his tone kindly endearing as she hugged him once more.

"Mama and Ajax taught me, but I want to learn more. Practice makes perfect, right?" she said, as Valen opened the journal and flipped to the first page, showing her a parchment with words scribbled out. He pointed to the first pair of words.

"Sweet fruits," he said, his voice a gentle whisper, showing her the individual letters and sounding them out. By the time Alana had finished with breakfast she knew the words for all the different flavors, and how to read Valen's mostly visual guide to the fruits, vegetables, and other foraged goods in the Feywilds. What she really appreciated was the entire chapter he showed her on the potentially hazardous flora.

"Eat up lass! Books later," Alana said in a sing-song manner, shoving the plate of blue meat, pink and white potatoes, and green yolk bearing eggs, which confused her, with a tap on her shoulder, followed by Valen pointing at a bird that was perched in a tree a good jog away. She'd never seen such a magnificent bird, even in the Royal Aviary. A dazzling display of greens and reds ran across its feathers, and it had a quite massive upright white frock. Before taking off, the bird let out a low, droning *squaw*. "Best eggs. Bird taste okay," Valen explained before diving into his plate. She followed suit, happy to stuff herself.

Alana was surprisingly polite, letting her rest after eating, as she took a brief nap against Valen. She was brimming with excitement to learn combat from Alana, as she stirred from her slumber and stretched her arms into the air with a quiet yawn.

"Yer ready, lass?" Alana asked, laying across the ground. Nova stood up and began walking around to shake away the sleepy feeling across her body.

"Yes! What am I learning?" Nova asked, pulling her hair back as Alana offered her a strip of leather to tie it up with.

"Me specialty lass, brawlin' on tha' ground an' grapplin'," Alana spoke while shooting up to her feet and walking alongside Nova to the patch of dirt.

"Shanti said to never be on the ground." Nova scrunched her face up, finding the differing instruction confusing.

Her current mentor let out a bellow of laughter. "Aye, lass. Ye should be keepin' yer arse off the ground. Ye get into 'nuff scraps and ye'll find tha floor. Just like tha pretty dirk o' yours'll find a belly. Better it be at yer side, and always stay tucked, than need it without havin' it aye?" Alana said as they stopped at the center of the exposed, torched dirt. Nova contemplated the vampiress' statement. Despite her rowdy demeanor, Nova realized that the drunken female was wiser than she outwardly portrayed.

"First lesson, lass, fightin' up close. Shanti already taught ye the stance," Alana exclaimed. Nova felt confused, yet she fell into the stance Shanti taught her. "We're nae learnin' like tha'. C'mere." Alana gestured for her to step in close. Without hesitation, she moved closer to her mentor, and Alana showed her the different places to grab and how to work with her weight, height, and strength. Within the first fifteen minutes, she'd successfully performed several techniques for throwing an opponent on Alana.

The taller dark-haired female laughed as she leapt to her feet from being sent soaring. "Fates lass, yer a bruiser. Yer a swift learner. Ye got throwin' now we'll find a few takedowns ye can manage. Legs work great, but if yer goin' against a lad like Valen, best ta be avoiding' trying ta bring em down. Watch. Valen! Bring yer mute arse over here!" Alana shouted out for the massive shifter, who landed in his typical plume of flames, changing from his winged phoenix form to the large and tender male she adored.

"Need help?" he asked, offering a polite wave as he jogged up to them.

"Aye, gon' teach tha' lass ta fight big oxen." Valen gave a

nod after Alana's explanation.

"Best chance, ye catch em from tha' back." Alana gestured to Valen's back before climbing him like a tree. "Take a gander at me legs." She pointed to her legs locked tight around Valen's waist. "Ye get tight where he cannae reach. Only problem is when ye get smashed into things. Never fun. Ye need to go fer tha' neck," Alana mentioned as she slipped from Valen's waist to her legs wrapped around his neck. "An' yer legs will be better fer choking 'em out." She squeezed her thighs together, crushing Valen's throat, until he tapped his hand against her thigh after his skin turned a pale blue and he began to sway toward the ground. Getting back to her feet Alana patted Nova's shoulder. "If ye can avoid it, don't fight big lads like Valen. Yer at a horrible disadvantage. Thank ya, yer free ta bugger off."

Valen gave a nod and stepped out of their training mound. Alana guided Nova through a variety of chokes, takedowns, and holds, and she showed her how to defend while pushing for any potential advantages. "Ye've got an expert knowledge now. Me last lessons are let no one control yer neck, an' watch every part of yer foes. Now we spar. Square off!" she said, just like Shanti, the words setting Nova into motion for the drilled stance.

Nova felt anxious knowing that Alana was more experienced, but she understood that she wasn't looking to harm her. She studied Alana's stance and stepped in between her legs, sliding forward into a knee, as she hooked her arms around both legs, and with all her might, lifted and slammed Alana into the ground.

Despite the immediate advantage, Alana slipped free, and

less than a second later, her muscular thighs were wrapped around Nova's throat. Struggling for breath, her chest ached as she attempted to pry Alana off her. Feeling defeated, she tapped Alana's side and freedom came as she sat up, taking a sharp inhale. "Fates…" She heaved for air.

"Yer doing good, lass. We'll get ye better than most. The rest'll come with practice," Alana said as she stuck her hand out and pulled Nova to her feet.

"Let's keep going!" Nova panted out as she stood up straight, before dropping into stance. The two spent a good chunk of the afternoon drilling a myriad of grappling and ground fighting techniques for defending and attacking.

⁂

After Alana's lessons in grappling, Nova spent her break meditating at the node, enjoying the peace that came from being far from any semblance of society. She'd truly loved being surrounded by the beauty of the lush and vibrant overgrowth of the untamed wilds. The more she trained, the more her yearning for adventure grew. Nova found great strength inside herself through her lessons, giving her insight into a word she'd never really understood before *confidence.*

She overheard Shanti and Alana talking in the distance on their way to the training mound, and she jogged to meet the two females, shooting out a question as the three came together. "We're doing blade training, right?"

"Aye lass, yer gon' watch fer now. Plant yer arse," Alana said, while pointing to a spot on the ground.

Nova fidgeted with her ring as she sat down and watched Shanti and Alana each pull a dagger free from their hips. She then followed closely as Alana demonstrated some defensive maneuvers with her dagger, and Shanti nearly slashed the brunette's head off dozens of times with her own displays.

With a foot to the chest, Shanti sent Alana onto her back with a dull grunt, and she held nothing back as she immediately dove on top of the vampiress, burying her dagger in the ground beside her ear. "Yer 'avin a piss!" Alana said, trying to push Shanti off, only to be met with a forearm crushing her throat.

"I think you're hurting her, Shanti…" Nova jumped to her feet, alarmed by the blueish haze tinting Alana's face.

"She's taken worse beatings," Shanti uttered callously as she stuck her finger in her mouth, only to jam the saliva covered digit into Alana's ear. Shanti was on her feet in the blink of an eye, the pride of triumph written across her strong features.

"Yer a bitch, lass!" Alana coughed out as she shoved her pinky into her ear to clear the remnants of Shanti's assault.

"Why did you do that to her?" Nova asked, picking up Alana's fallen dagger.

"Punishment. She knows why," Shanti said, yanking her own dagger free from the soil. "Attack me!" the lycaness commanded, tossing her blade up and catching it by the tip.

"How?" Nova asked, falling into a defensive stance, unsure of exactly what to do next.

"Find an opening, lass," Alana grumbled out from the

sidelines, as Nova studied Shanti, searching for a way to strike her. Taking the knife firmly in her hand, she charged at Shanti, who effortlessly jabbed her in the throat with the blunted end of the handle on her dagger. "You're dead," she said, idly staring at her nails as Nova caught her footing. "What if I stab you?" Nova asked while flipping the blade to a reverse grip.

"You stab me and I'll carry you on my shoulders all the way to the damned Court," replied Shanti, before tucking her own dagger away and dropping her hands to her sides. Nova stepped toward her, avoiding the first punch, and as her knife came down in a swift arc toward Shanti's body, she snatched Nova's wrist in mid-air and flipped her onto her back. "Aggressive for a rookie. You're not ready for reverse grip." With a yank, Shanti pulled Nova to her feet. "Drill defense with Alana," Shanti said as she turned her back to Nova and took off toward the colorful tree line of the Feywilds.

Alana reached her hand out to Nova." Oi lass! Mi arse took a nap!" Nova hesitated before clasping palms with the brunette and pulling her upright, then Alana strolled about as Nova took her dagger from the leather sheath. The brunette pulled a thick stick from the grass and rushed at Nova, slapping it against her calf. "Ow! You could have warned me!" Nova shouted as she slipped into a defensive stance.

"Cannae be a wee baby lass. Ye never know when something may come fer yer 'ead, aye?" Alana said as she caught Nova's side with a jab. Nova's attempted parry was too slow as the stab of pain in her ribs caused her to step back.

"Five seconds lass," Alana's warning came as Nova gathered her thoughts. She took a deep inhale and suddenly felt connected with the world around her. The whistle of the stick soared at Nova, but with a precise swipe her blade collided with it, slicing a finger length chunk off. "Ya got yer head on right lass!" The assault kept coming. At first, Nova missed every other parry, but after several strikes to the side and legs, she cleaved any shot Alana sent her way. Thinking back to Shanti's first lessons, she leaned into dodging and parrying the vampiress' assault skillfully. Alana's motivating cheers of praise kept Nova going until Alana eventually dropped her last stick cut to the same length as a small knife. "Good job, lass, ye 'ave cat's feet. It'll keep ya alive."

"Enough coddling!" Shanti said, her voice a startling boom as she threw Alana toward the tree line.

Nova tracked the burly woman's flight, until a harsh jab against her forehead drew her focus to the tall blonde. "What do you mean?"

Shanti's silence set her nerves on edge, then, within the blink of an eye, a slice split her cheek, blood now coating most of her face.

With a shift of her feet and a defensive brandishing of her dagger, Nova's eyes fixated on Shanti's well-toned body. A stab thrust toward her chest was met with a sidestep and her own hand, sending her blade in an arc toward Shanti's shoulder.

As Nova's blade bit into the targeted muscle, Shanti buried her own in Nova's side, the pain blooming a moment later, causing her to drop. "You stabbed me!" she screeched out, tucking her hand against the gash.

"Merely a flesh wound," Shanti dismissed, yanking her blade free before darting into the dense woods.

Nova whimpered as she held back the urge to cry, blood rushing from the freshly made tear across her flesh. Her breathing was erratic, and she couldn't find a shred of focus to call upon her magic. "I… can't stop it."

With each passing moment, she grew colder, the soil greedily soaking up her blood. After all her work, would her demise be from Shanti's crude training? She couldn't understand why Shanti would leave her injured. Her waning life had her mind swimming aimlessly.

Steadying her breathing was the first mountain to climb, as she recalled Ajax's lessons. A passing minute of controlling each breath felt akin to years. Using the technique shown to her, she found a glimmer of focus as she pressed her hand against the flesh. Every thought in her mind fixed on the flesh of her side, pulling together as her hand burst alive with a vibrant blue glow, the pain easing with each second as her wound slowly re-knit itself, leaving the flesh looking unmarked.

"You did it. You saved yourself. Better to be your own savior than wait for one," Shanti stated from behind her.

Nova's eyes narrowed into thin slits, as she felt wrath riding across her body. "That was cruel! You left me for dead!" she shouted.

"You would never have died." Shanti turned her eyes away, before her strong fingers snapped at gripping Nova's throat.

"Yell at me again and I'll teach you what death feels like," she said, the threat enough to have Nova raising her hands in defeat. "Don't get into a knife fight if you can help it," she warned before pulling her hand from Nova's throat.

Nova filled her lungs with a deep breath. She felt ashamed that her efforts over the last couple of hours meant nothing. "Is any of my fighting good?" she whispered out, nervous to hear Shanti's answer.

"No. It's all terrible, but you've only had a day to learn," Shanti said as she sat against the ground, her legs crossed over each other. "Sit with me," the lycaness commanded.

Nova did as told; only a hand's length separating them. "So why teach me anything? Why can't you and Alana handle the fighting?" she asked, her copper eyes locked on Shanti, studying her sharp emerald gaze.

"You won't always have us. Anything can happen," Shanti said as the wind picked up, blowing her shoulder blade length blonde hair with it. "The lessons don't stop when we start the journey. I'm an old bitch and I've still got lessons to learn."

"What else must I learn? Teach me before we go," Nova said, unsure of her own words in this moment.

"Hunting, stealth, foraging, and plenty more. You'll learn, or you won't eat," Shanti said, with a push to her feet, and her back now turned to face the sun as it dipped below the horizon. "Relax for the evening. You might be a shit fighter, but you've got potential. We'll work on it along the way."

"Could I be like you one day?" Nova asked, the concept of being awe-inspiring like Shanti urged her to face the sun's descent.

"No," Shanti said. Any ego built over the last few days deflated as doubt consumed Nova's thoughts. "That doesn't mean you will never become a force to be reckoned with," she stated, her hands cupping Nova's cheeks. "You're Nova'ivar, not Shanti Odin's-Eye. There's only one of you in this lifetime. Don't waste yourself emulating a crank like me." Shanti's grin, despite her self-depreciating comment, left Nova puzzled.

"I don't want to be me, though. I've spent my life as little more than a toy," Nova said, her hands covering Shanti's. The warm touch was deceptive, given Shanti's typically crass demeanor. "No one has ever treated you like me. You're too strong for that…" she whimpered out as she dropped her eyes.

A laughter burst out from Shanti's lips, before her hand moved to slap against Nova's shoulder, leaving a dull sting. "Fates, if only that were true," she grumbled out, shaking her head.

Nova contemplated who might have the power to treat Shanti as a meaningless slave, but she was unable to conjure anything less than a god's visage as one who could overpower such a proud female. "How? Who?" she mumbled to herself, an answer not something she expected.

"My father. I found strength when I tore his throat out and ate his heart," Shanti said, not an inkling of humor across her face. As Nova was about to apologize for the horrors inflicted upon Shanti, the blonde clapped her hand over Nova's mouth. "I don't need your condolences. Fucker's been dead for eons. I have his skull for proof," she stated before rising and moving to the woods. "I'm going for a run. You're done for today. Relax. You won't get to again for a while after tonight and tomorrow."

As the blonde took off, her form contorted rapidly into a four-legged beast. Thick, golden white fur sprouted across her body as she dropped to all fours. Powerful muscles rippled beneath the coat of the creature, its shoulders standing nearly as tall as Shanti's human height, with sharp upward pointing ears. Nova gazed in awe at the massive beast. Shanti's animal form embodied the savage strength of her warrior spirit. With a shake of her fur, the giant beast bounded off into the darkness of the woods, her footfalls fading into the distance.

CHAPTER 13

CAMARADERIE

Nova rose from her slumber, the morning sun catching her face, leaving her skin warmed by its rays until something blocked the sight of the orange and blue blazing hues. She peeled her eyes open to see Valen's hand outstretched to act as a shield. She clutched his tunic and dragged herself upward to plant a kiss on his cheek. "Good morning, Valen. Did you sleep?" she asked as she sat up while rubbing at her eyes.

He gave her a nod as he sat up alongside her. "Yes. Not enough," he said with a gruff smile behind his untamed mustache. She reached out to spear her fingers into the hair that covered much of his face and dangled low to his chest. The weight of him leaning his head into her palms made her cheeks ache from the smile running across her face.

"Did I move around too much?" She studied his features, wondering at the mysteries that lay deep in his heart. What had left the scars he bore in silence?

Valen shook his head as he patted the top of her own with his heavy hand. "No. Never sleep well," he muttered as he offered her a one-armed shrug. "Day of rest before adventure. What Nova do?" He scratched his nails against the top of her scalp ever so gently. She found the same rumble that had come from her drunken nuzzles toward Alana, roaring forth. "Purr cute." His words came out as the softest of whispers.

Her face heated intensely as her eyes darted away from his. "Thank you. I'm not sure. What do you do before an adventure?" Nova shifted to sit on one of his legs and leaned her back against him while staring upwards at the sky.

"Meditate, rest," he instructed her as he tapped the side of his skull with one of his fingers, and his other hand moved to cover where his heart was. "Seek center."

Nova ran her fingers through his beard. "How do I know when I've found it?" She shut her eyes, despite the coarse texture of the hairs. She found the sensation of the strands running through her fingers soothing.

"Center not found. Center, calm within storms," Valen said as Nova laid back down, leaning into him with all her weight. Her mind raced with trying to understand what he meant. Why did he always leave her with more questions than answers? She knew what he said carried depth and wisdom. If only she could understand it.

Alana placed a bowl of soup in her hands. "Git something in yer belly! Tha day's jus' begun!" she cheered out while sitting beside the two of them, sipping from her own bowl.

"Alana, what do you do the last day before a journey?" Nova asked before drawing on the savory and heart-warming burst of flavor from the bowl.

The vampiress shrugged her shoulders. "Nae much lass, mayhap flick tha bean, aye. Sleep lots. Shanti ain't one fer stopping ta camp often." Alana glared at the tall blonde in the distance with a rueful gaze.

"Flick the bean?" Nova rubbed her chin inquisitively, as Valen gave a gentle knock to the top of Alana's head with a hammered strike from the side of his hand.

The brunette shoved his side, but he remained immovable. "Oi keep yer mittens off me ya lummox! Lass is missing out! Flicking tha bean's me favorite pastime!" She flashed Nova a lopsided and coy grin.

"What does it mean?" Nova asked aloud, finding herself fearful of the answer, given Valen's protective strike against Alana.

Valen patted Novas's head before wrapping his arms around her. "No worry. Alana ridiculous," he said as she felt his heat curl around her. It was such an intoxicating sensation.

"More like a complete dumbass." Shanti dropped into a cross-legged seated position in front of them. "Don't let her corrupt your mind. She lost her own to the bottle ages ago," she warned her before clapping her hand against her shoulder. "Enjoy the last day of peace. It might be your last. Keep that in mind. Whether you want to squat under a tree like a punk while humming and chanting, drink until you strip naked, or sleep the day away. It's yours. Don't let any of us tell you how to take it easy," The blonde pulled out a pouch of pungent weeds, stuffing them into her mouth.

With Shanti's disruption, the group fell silent, all taking to their breakfast without a word. With each sip of her bowl, a distant whisper trailed through the air. Something *familiar*. A beckon tugging at her ring, making it difficult to stay seated as she worried the ring might fly off her finger.

Nova stood up after finishing her soup, handing the bowl to Alana, and bid a quick farewell before darting off to the node, following the pulling force at her hand, and the coo in her ear. Taking her place beneath the mushroom, she sprouted back to life, leaning her back against the dense stalk. She shut her eyes and allowed the sound of the whisper to enthrall her. She knew it to be a hazardous venture, yet the desire to *listen* and give way to that which called upon solely her was a curiosity she needed to date.

At first, she tracked the flow of each breath, fixating on how she took in or put out energy with each controlled gust of wind into her lungs. A slow draw through the nose, before holding it deep, feeling the tingle of her chest absorbing, not just that which she needed with each breath, but the very life within the Ether. With an unknown passage of time, her breathing found a steady tempo that kept in pace with the world around her.

With her hands curled together in the center of the triangle formed by her legs, she spun her ring in a slow, languid motion. Even if it were only her finger, she liked to imagine her mother hugged her vicariously through the copper band. Whispers grew louder with each full revolution. The sensation of the engraving on the inside of the band, which read out something beyond her understanding, grazed along her skin.

She opened her eyes as a warmth fell upon her hand and cheek. The touch of fingertips away as standing before her was a specter of a past long gone. A vision she was certain was the Ether playing tricks on her mind, yet the whispers that turned to the sweetest coo, a sound she yearned across the centuries to hear, as her eyes traced the petite yet tall frame, matched not with simple slave's garments, but an elaborate visage of elegance beyond even Ajax's tastes. Symbols of the Moon in silver and gold thread spun in a tapestry dedicated to Buwan adorned every inch of her, with rich blue hair and eyes to match her own. Her face held a slenderer appearance, and her eyes a sharp brilliance beyond that which she recalled rested in her mama's eyes.

"My sweet Nova… look at you," Sela'mann uttered with a hitched voice as she kneeled to cup both of Nova's cheeks and flashed her a wide smile. "I'm so proud of you, setting forth where I failed to take the first steps. If only I'd taken up the journey when your father offered…I might have given you a better life."

Nova leaned into the touch of the spectral hand, and her eyes began to sting as she shut them, hoping to hide the tears that threatened to fall. Her mother reached out to brush them away. "My father? You never told me about him," Nova said, as Sela sat beside her and enveloped her in her translucent arms.

"You're right. I'm sorry, my sweet Nova. I thought I was protecting you," Sela cooed out as she squeezed her even tighter. "I wish I could tell you everything, but we only have a few moments. Find your way home. I can tell you everything from there. You deserve so much better than I could give you, my love."

Nova reached out to grasp her mother's hand. "I can see you in the Moon Court?"

Sela nodded and laughed as she rubbed her nose to Nova's. "Yes. I can hold form there. The magic of the Seelie Court had cut us off from Buwan's blessings. We are not fae of light, we are children of the Moons. Shanti and Alana can get you to the Court. You must purge the filth that has taken up residence in the halls. Then I can come home to you."

Nova smiled as she felt the tears of joy run down her cheeks. "I won't let you down," she said as her mother's form began to drift away after one last kiss to her forehead.

"You are Buwan's light taken form." Sela's last words left Nova with an even deeper hole in her heart. Yet within the cored-out center in her chest, there laid a burning heat to ensure she would not disappoint her mother and the goddess.

The whispers faded as Nova opened her eyes, the specter of her mother gone. She sat in contemplative silence, watching the shafts of sunlight stretch across the vibrant meadow. Nova felt changed after her encounter, as if a missing piece of herself had clicked into place. The determination to make her mother proud now burned within.

As the sun dipped below the horizon, Nova set about preparing for the next day's departure. She took stock of her equipment and practiced skills Shanti and Alana had taught her, feeling more confident in her abilities. Inside, nervous excitement churned about the journey ahead into the unknown.

When dusk fell, Nova made her way back to the camp. Valen had returned and was using his fiery breath to build up the campfire. The flickering flames cast dancing shadows across his massive frame. Nova smiled at the sight of her gentle, giant companion. Alana soon joined them, singing a soft and lively drinking tune in her thick brogue.

The group gathered around the crackling fire as darkness swallowed the vibrant wilderness around them. Shanti dropped with an audible *thud* beside her and wrapped her muscular arm around her neck. "I'm proud of ya. Ya know that? A few days ago, you were a helpless whelp doomed to death. Now? You'll survive and you got enough of a clue to adapt.

Nova turned her eyes upward to match Shanti's emerald orbs. "You really think I've got it in me to get through all this?" she asked, trying to not squeal with glee, knowing Shanti felt pride in her.

"Hell yeah, sister. I know it. I know even if something steps on the drunk cunt and I, you'll be all right. Ain't much other than the giants in the Feywilds you can't handle now if you put your mind to it. You only need three words to keep moving. What are they, ya runt?" Shanti asked as she released Nova and grinned, clapping her hand roughly against the small of her back.

Nova sat up straight as the sting sprawled across her back, keeping her eruption of pain to herself. "Survive, adapt, thrive!" She cheered out the mantra on constant repeat in her mind after all her training.

"Atta' fucking girl! How was your commune with nature or whatever ya do when sitting around all magical and whatnot?" Shanti asked as she snatched the bottle tucked between Alana's legs and took a hearty pull on it.

Nova shrugged her shoulders, unsure if she should discuss her conversation with her mother. She liked the idea of keeping that private. "Just focus on everything I've learned, and center my mind, spirit, and body," she said as she took the bottle from Shanti and sucked down a mouthful. When she offered it to Valen, he declined with a wave of his hand. Her mind swirled pleasantly from the brew, and a tingle of warmth spread out from her belly.

"Mm, sounds boring. I'd rather knock teeth out, or hunt," Shanti said as she reached out for one of the raw steaks beside Valen, sinking her teeth into it.

Nova let out a low chuckle as she nudged herself closer to the massive male. "I suppose it could bore, but I think you have to be a little bored to get good at magic?" she asked as the scent of the steaks being laid on a clean, ripping hot slate of rock atop the fire hit her nose. Her stomach churned as she realized just how empty it felt.

"Why that is not too far off from the truth, Nova'ivar," Ajax said as he appeared behind her. Before Nova could react, he held out a small wooden plate with something on it. A dark-colored cake. "A sweet to congratulate your efforts. You have exceeded expectations in every way, Nova. The journey ahead is perilous. I would hope when you find yourself lost along the way, these few evenings of camaraderie give you light through the darkness." Ajax settled the cake on her lap.

She stared down at the cake, awe-struck not by the treat itself but the gravity of Ajax's kindness; a male who myth painted as the vilest of villains to cross the annals of fae history had only continually uplifted her. "Thank you… all of you." She fought to keep the tears in her eyes as a mere mist.

"It's been a pleasure showing ye how tae pick yerself up after falling doon. Yer a tough lassie. Now settle yer arse and eat yer cake. I'll tell ye aboot the time Shanti and I hunted ducks tha' were three times the size o' Valen!" Alana said as she hopped to her feet, excitement to spin her tale dancing within her husky eyes.

Nova propped herself up against Valen, fixating solely on Alana, as she began digging into the cake with her hands, offering Valen a sizeable chunk, which he graciously took.

"Closer to two. Alana can't tell her ass from a hole in the

ground," Shanti grumbled as she took up a spot on the other side of Valen. It seemed odd. She hadn't seen Shanti show physical affection like that before, and yet she understood that if she had to pick one person to trust herself to be wholly vulnerable with, it would be Valen every time. It was his endearing eyes. They gave a silent vow he would be tender with the most fragile parts of her spirit.

"Oi! Put yer fist in yer gob ya cunt, I'm telling stories!" Alana snapped out as she stepped behind the fire so it illuminated her wild hair splayed out, standing unpredictably. Her speckled, constantly flushed cheeks caught the warm glow so majestically that Nova had just truly seen the beauty behind Alana for the first time.

The campfire crackled, casting flickering shadows across Alana's face. The vampiress flashed a roguish grin, clearly reveling in the captive audience.

"It was a dark n' stormy night when me and Shanti set sail fer the cursed isle." Alana waved her hands dramatically, painting the scene. "The seas tossed our wee plank about like a leaf! *'Hold yer britches!'* I shouted, as freezing walls o' water crashed over tha deck."

Nova leaned forward, enraptured by the tale, hanging on the vampiress' every word, as she set her hand on Valen's leg to know she had some security, even if Alana's tale grew horrifying.

"The jagged rocks looked ready tae rip our hull apart!" Alana mimed vicious claws with her fingernails. "But somehow we made it tae the shore, soaked n' shiverin, dinghy destroyed yet our bellies set on eating tha big duckies," Alana explained as she flared her hands.

Her voice dropped low. "Then... out came the beasts. Ducks so big ol' Valen 'ere woulda been a wee lad; with teeth like daggers! Nearly lost me tits!" Valen rumbled amusement at being incorporated into the grandiose tale, but simply ran his fingers through Nova's hair.

"We merry bitches drew our blades. What 'appens next... och, that's a tale fer next camp, lassie!" Alana winked, taking a triumphant swig of her brew.

Nova scowled and settled back against Valen, erupting in laughter as Shanti beamed Alana between the eyes with her boot, taking the vampiress down. "At least have the honor of finishing a story once you start it."

"Oi… ow tha hurt…" Alana groaned out as she rubbed at her forehead, getting to her feet. "Ye jus' wan' me ta spin tales of ya savin' me sorry arse! Glory hogging wench!"

Shanti snorted out as she rose to her feet. Stepping to where Alana stood, she kicked Alana in the center of her chest and sent the vampiress onto her ass. "I'll finish because the drunk clearly can't. We hunted down all those stupid birds; ate most of them. Fuckers were good. When we found the biggest one, Alana here thought she could go at it with her busted up knuckles and a kilt. Had to cut her out of the damn thing's belly. Worst part is its guts smelled better than she does." Shanti babbled out quickly before sitting beside Valen once more.

"I don' smell!" Alana screeched out in horror. "Yer breath's backing up on ya again!" she retorted, only for Shanti's other boot to be the lycaness' response. Alana had avoided catching another heel to the forehead, as she swatted the boot right into the fire. "Ah! Ye ain't got boots now!" she cackled out, all the while sticking her pink tongue out.

Nova couldn't resist but join in with Alana's uproar as Shanti dove over the flames to pounce on Alana, tearing her boots off and throwing them into the fire. "And yours are on fire," Shanti snarled out as she returned to the opposing side of Valen.

"My uncouth as ever, Shanti," Ajax said as he offered Alana his hand.

Shanti scoffed out as she kicked her feet up onto Valen's knee. "Couth is for the weak. When hard times come, the soft die out," she stated.

"Aye, yer nae wrong ye ain', ain't gotta always be wailin' on me! Taken 'nuff lumps in me life…" Alana grumbled out as she stood up with Ajax's aide. "Laddie, can ye conjure me up new boots?" she asked, turning an almost cherub plead in her eyes toward Ajax.

"As you wish," Ajax said as he moved to squat beside Nova. "Would you like to watch? Perhaps take part in it?" he asked, turning his keen gaze upon her as she locked her eyes with his. He was capable of kindness and compassion when all she could think of when their eyes matched the sensation of a splendid beast about to swallow her whole.

"Yes!" Nova stood up so fast her heart skipped a beat. When Ajax held his hands out to her, she hovered hers above them. She noted how unmarred his hands were, so smooth compared to Shanti, Valen, or Alana.

A soft violet light billowed out from the lines across Ajax's hands, and she channeled her own to match it as she shut her eyes to feel how Ajax would conjure the boot.

With graceful movements, Ajax began looping violet threads into the faint shape of a pair of boots. Nova poured her energy toward him, sensing the complex magic required for such a task.

Ajax deftly manipulated the glowing laces, crafting them into an intricate pattern down the boot's side. Nova studied the way Ajax moved, how he'd sculpt each individual detail with the tips of his fingers, each one acting as an individual quill.

With a last flourish, the spectral boot solidified into tangible leather form. Ajax held up their creation, the firelight dancing across the polished leather. "A fine pair for the journey." He offered them to Alana.

Alana sat on the ground and tucked her feet into the new boots. She then hopped to her feet and took off in a blinding dash of speed, leaving a wake of wind rushing behind her. "These're tha best me feet's ever worn! Yer knife ear magic is something else." She plopped down in the same place she sat before.

"How long did it take you to get your magic to that level Ajax?" Nova asked, as she leaned back against Valen.

Ajax brushed his hands along his robes, a dusting of his magic, cleaning any dirt from crouching. "It wasn't a matter of time. It is a willingness to sell one's soul," he stated in a manner that left Nova with her eyes lost in the dancing flames.

"Oh… I don't want to be that powerful…" She hugged her knees to her chest. She wanted to be as magically adept as her mentor, but what sacrifices had he made in the name of power? "Do you regret it?" she asked, afraid of the revelation.

"One cannot regret the choices others foist upon them. You know this all too well." Ajax turned his back to head to his cabin. "I shall see you in the morning, Nova. Do not go rushing off without speaking to me." With that Ajax was gone, and Nova lowered her eyes to her feet, falling into silent contemplation.

"Good. Time for bed. I'm sick of looking at all your sorry mugs," Shanti said as she stood up from Valen's side and walked over to the leather bedroll she had, laying out and shutting her eyes.

Alana smiled at Nova and leaned over to wrap her arms around her shoulders. "Aye lass, yer a tough nut. Proud of ye. Rest up!" she cheered out before heading to her bedroll. "Sweet slumber! Don't let crawlin' critters chomp on yer hide!"

With only her and Valen staring at the crackling flames, she moved to take her place in the triangular crevice created by his crossed legs. She curled her knees to her chest so she could fit snuggly, without disturbing his comfort, with her head now resting back against his belly, staring up at him. The stray hairs of his coarse beard gently grazed her forehead. "Can we stay up a little longer before we go to bed?" she asked in a low voice to avoid disturbing Shanti.

He gave her a silent nod as he encased her with his arms over his legs, curling his massive body over her own. "Can we sit together like this when I come back?" she asked, hopeful that her journey wouldn't change their relationship. She reached out to take both of his hands with her own.

He gave a shake of his head before lightly squeezing her hands. "Yes. If Nova wants." He flashed her that smile buried beneath untamed facial hair, and she reached her hand up to brush the hair covering his lips away and returned the expression.

"You have the prettiest smile, Valen… why do you hide it?" she asked as she nuzzled her head against him.

He gave a shrug of his shoulders before averting his gaze from her. The exposed skin of his cheeks took on a faint reddish hue. "Thank you," he said with an aching doubt to his words.

Nova moved to stand up, now matching Valen's eyes with her own. "You truly are beautiful, even if you can't see it," she said in her most tender voice as she cupped his cheeks, using her thumbs to keep the hair parted from his lips. After a long moment of admiring the male, she leaned in to wrap her arms around his neck, squeezing tightly. "The realms don't deserve you," she whispered against his ear as she felt his arms loop around her pressing her into him.

Valen scooped Nova up as she drifted off in their embrace, even with all the food and blood she'd been given, she was so tiny in his arms. He wished he had the words to explain the rapture he felt in watching her flourish over the last few days. In what was a blink of an eye for him, she sprouted. From the sensitive, beaten-down victim, to finding her own fight worth raising arms for, and unleashing her inner strength. Her distance would leave him worried for her safety, yet he knew she would return. He wondered who she would be at the end of her first journey. What parts of herself would she uncover?

He moved gingerly, to avoid making a sound as he brought Nova to the bedroll. He laid down without breaking their contact. "Feed. Need blood before journey," he uttered as he reached up to pull his beard away from his neck, clearing space for her to bite into his neck easily. The stiff wind against his weathered skin was a soothing sensation he hadn't felt in some time.

"I'm okay, Valen. I've fed a lot already," Nova said, as she nestled herself closer to him. "Thank you for offering. I just… I feel like a monster when I do it," she mumbled out as her warm, metallic eyes dropped, shame scrawled across her face. That look felt like a dagger being yanked back and forth in his stomach.

With a grumble, he shifted her so her head was near the exposed flesh. "Not monster. Need blood to live. Eat meat to live. Cycle of life," he spoke in as soft of a tone as he could muster. He knew better than to let her have her way. He wanted to send her off with every advantage for her pilgrimage.

"Valen, stop. I hate feeding. Please. You have those scars… I know what they mean. You don't have to put yourself through that again for me. I'd rather never feed again. It feels like I'm sucking the life out of you, and when there's a part of me that loves taking from you, I realize how terrible I truly am," Nova uttered as she moved out of his grasp. Her back turned to him as she sat up. "It's one thing to do it to animals, but to you? You deserve better," she said, letting out an exacerbated sigh at the end of her statement.

Valen moved closer to Nova, sitting up with a hand on her shoulder, then his weary eyes traced the waves of her deep blue hair. He loved to touch it so much when she would let him. "Want to. Like giving. Only blood. Body makes more. Nova, not monster, survivor," he said, wishing Shanti or Alana would step in. He knew they were awake. Sensing the pulses of the flickering flames of their souls, he could feel their focus upon them. Yet, knowing Shanti, this was one of her *tests* for him. Her way of *sticking my foot in your ass when you need it.* The words of one of his oldest companions rang across his skull.

Nova let out a sigh as she spun around to face him, tears welling up in her eyes. The very sight caused a deep stabbing sensation to fill his chest. He clenched his fists. The echoes of her past would always haunt her. He knew it all too well. His own still found their way to torment him, even after eons. "I know you're trying to just show me love and take care of me… I know it's what you want to do Valen, but I hate taking like that from you. It hurts you." She spoke with her voice crackling along the way.

"It does?" he asked, finding himself confused at how she came along to that assumption. He rubbed the side of his head and let out a nervous chuckle. That had guilt spearing him in the gut for showing a sign of amusement while she was distraught. "Feels good. Like venom and bites."

Nova looked at him, her tears ceasing immediately with her brows furrowed in confusion. "You like it? How? I'm sucking the life out of you!" she let out loud enough that Shanti sent a rock their way.

"Just blood. Life not just blood," he said as he patted the top of her head gently. "Yes, feel good. Promise." He brought his free hand to adjust his beard to clear space for her to feed again. "Can feed now?" he asked.

"Fine…" Nova moved to bring herself closer to his neck. She let out a sigh, her breath tickling his skin before he felt her rubbing her nose along his vein. He sat perfectly still, keeping every muscle and joint frozen. He shut his eyes as he felt her sink her fangs into his flesh. The quick sting of her twin fangs was a jolt that ran down to his spine to between his legs.

Her venom was barely noticeable, yet it felt like a kiss across every inch of his body. He liked the sensation, even if he had to adjust his leg so he would avoid prodding her with something she surely would have no desire for. He found it endearing how, instead of chugging, she allowed his blood to flow freely. All the while the faint crackles of the campfire to lulled him into a deep state of peace.

Once her belly was full, she leaned back. The twin marks on his neck healed after only a single droplet from each raced down his neck until Nova caught them with her fingers. "Thank you, Valen," she whispered out to him, her delicate fangs peeking out as she spoke. She moved to lie down across the center of their bedroll. "One last night together? Gonna be hard sleeping without you…" she mumbled out as he curled around her.

He shushed her as he let his fingers run through her hair.

When she erupted in a tenderly affectionate rumble as she nuzzled the back of her head against his palm, he grinned madly. These were the type of moments he would often think of. The ones that kept the flame within alive through the turmoil of eons. The strife and havoc that his life had always entailed. He would give anything to spend an epoch or two in this sort of comfort. Even if it called for him to shift his legs to conceal the involuntary hardening.

The rolling purr ceased from Nova's chest, quickly replaced by the softest of sounds. It was less like snoring and more a heavy breathing, the faintest whisper of air moving through her nose the only sound to fill their otherwise motionless campsite. Even the fire smoldered into dormancy.

He laid restlessly through the evening, his mind wandering in every which direction. Starting with worrying about every individual danger Nova might face, even though Shanti and Alana could bring most foes to their knees, he worried they should have given Nova more training. Yet Ajax was insistent on the timeline. Not once had he been wrong.

Even when he'd shift focus to the upcoming appearances with Ajax, he wondered why he was the preferred companion for such a male. Not that he minded. Ajax had always proven he aligned his goals with justice, even if his methods were questionable.

Following Ajax had allowed Valen to explore the cuisines of the Realms. He particularly liked the spicier foods of the Eastern Terran regions. He wondered if Nova might like those same things, or would her taste be more delicate?

He'd spent the rest of the evening mentally plotting all the foods he'd make for Nova upon her return. Desserts, from custards to cakes, soups and stews of every beast, platters and mountains of different entrees until she'd eat so much, she'd lament a fear of her belly bursting. All the while, her most lovely smile beaming so brilliantly it would blind him. The musings of another life, he supposed. Maybe if they were born human, and had met, enjoying a few brief decades together before cycling through again. He envied it, to experience the cycles of life, death, and all the countless paths a soul might take. Fate excluded him from those cycles. He wondered if that was why he laid alone most nights. Had he been through many cycles of life even before these uncountable eons of chaos?

By the time he'd finally drifted off, Shanti was awake and checking her gear, which ruined any opportunity of sleep for at least two days.

SNEAK PEEK

A deep and blissful slumber ripped away as only a sea of darkness filled her vision. Hitched breathing and hushed sobs, far off in the distance breaking the dreadful silence, caught her attention. There laid a feminine figure with the handle of Nova's dagger that stood upright from her midsection.

She took off toward the figure. With each step closer, more features became distinguishable. Skin pale as the Moon wrapped around the handle of the blade, and the unmistakable mass of dark blue hair, much like her own, had her belly flooded with tension.

She dropped to her knees beside the figure. Her worst fear had come true. The person she loved more than the world itself, her own mother falling to the cruel hand of fate. Rivers of tears ran down her cheeks as she stared across a mangled body. "Mama..." she whispered out, fearful that she'd get a lifeless silence.

"My Nova," Sela'mann uttered as her hand came to Nova's cheek, a trembled touch, as raising her arm called forth more energy than she could spare. "Oh, no darling… you shouldn't be here," she spoke, before her hand dropped as a violent cough racked through her, spraying blood outward.

Nova clutched her mother's hand in her own, bringing the palm against her cheek once more, then she shook her head, the rush of tears only worsening as the darkness seemed to pull away. A flash of light showed the throne room… moments later came a crash matching only the wrath of gods. A pool of blood surrounded the two of them and drenched her legs. "Please stay with me, Mama!" Nova roared out.

"I can't…" Her mother's voice grew weaker with each syllable. She drew in a shallow breath, a droning wheeze alongside it. "I would give anything to stay, my love. Sadly, fate has other plans."

"Mama…" Nova whimpered out, unable to even string together another thought as the terror of being without the love and guidance of her mother left her feeling hopeless.

"Before Fate claims me, I need you to listen," Sela declared, her voice a hoarse whisper. "I have shown you my ring. You must guard it with your life, as I have done. He will kill you if he finds it. Buwan will guide you to it when only her light fills the—"

A dull thud of a body dropping beside Sela ended her statement. Nova's eyes shot to the figure, spotting the broch that signified the heir to the throne, Prince Rys. The master who had only ever shown her and her mother kindness was now a mangled husk.

From the shadows, a hand speared into her hair and clenched with a violent yank, sending her tumbling into one of the nearby pillars. Nova's screech of agony that followed left her throat hoarse. The darkness returned, consuming the throne room, and Prince Rys in its wake.

A male stood over her mother, hand clenched around her throat and another at the dagger in her belly, jerking it about, a brief agonized wail sounding out from her mother's lips, ceasing only when her face slumped against the ground. The hand at her mother's neck moved to the collar of her nightgown. The sound of fabric being torn sent Nova spiraling to consciousness.

Nova shot awake from the horrors buried deep within her memories, the last image of her mother's lifeless copper eyes, matched with the sound of fabric tearing.

Her hand clutched to her mouth as she pushed to her feet and sprinted away from Valen to brace her arms against a tree for support as she hunched over, a rush of vomit emptying the remnants of yet-to-be-digested dinner from the evening prior across the multi-colored grass. All she could manage was retching and heaving. Even after her belly turned, she gagged on the air that came with her body's endless purging.

When the tidal wave of illness let up, she moved to the other side of the tree and collapsed, sobbing as she could not wipe away visions of her mother's last moments.

All the years of Prince Thazin's cruelty piled over the horrific memory her freedom had unearthed.

A familiar touch of the past enveloped her hand. The stroke

of a silky-smooth feminine thumb moved along the finger that bore her mother's ring. Distant whispers beckoned her deep into the Feywilds, a tender coo that instinctively drew her to spin her ring. She turned her eyes to greet the comforting touch, only to find that she was alone. Pulling her knees to her chest and slinging her arms around them, she wept, burying her face in her thighs.

When her tears ran dry, the soft sobs drifted into silence. Doubt flooded every path of thought. All she could envision was her own failure, leaving those who had put their faith in her disappointed. Horrified at the idea of winding up as her mother had.

Survive, adapt, thrive. Shanti's mantra echoed out in the sea of despair that consumed her, catching her attention. She had no choice in turning back and running away, seeking a soft life. Something deep within had her yearning to find her ancestral Court. To keep the Court of Moons' history from being forgotten.

Nova spat the grime that accumulated in her mouth onto the ground and took off at a sprint toward the node. She noted everyone hadn't moved from their spots on the ground, Shanti and Alana near the fire.

The blonde having been sitting upright with her eyes peeled open, the only one who laid awake besides Nova. She could feel the hard gaze on her back, her mind drifting to Valen and the giant male's inspiring wisdom. Resolute in being just as strong as the group of people she loved as the family her heart yearned for across the centuries of torment.

Her jog halted at the center of the node. With a slow inhale through her nose, stretching her chest out as her lungs filled to the brim with air, she held her breath in for several moments before letting it free through her lips in a controlled, focused stream for as long as she'd held it. The burning in her throat from the prior emptying of her belly at first was a distraction. More methodical breathing, and the sensation dulled into a faint buzz.

Focus swept over her, and she drew the dagger that took her mother's life. Revolted that she'd bound herself to it, every racing thought in her mind now fixated on the blade and finding its destruction to seek her own vengeance. Her eyes locked on the dark red line that ran along its center.

She imagined it turning to ash at a faint touch, just as Ajax had displayed during his lessons. Flowing her own mana along with tapping into the node for the very power of the Ether, the clear crystalline metal took on a sharp blue and red glow with both her hands wrapped around the handle. The light grew so bright she couldn't even make out her own hands within it.

Of all things she'd expected to happen, she hadn't imagined the blinding flash and burst of mana that sent her tumbling into the hard-wooded log wall of Ajax's cabin. The world around her fell into darkness the moment her head collided against rough bark.

A soft violet plume of light against her eyelids filled the darkness as consciousness rushed back to her. Her last memory was being propelled through the air. Her hand came to clutch the achiest spot in her head. A low, pained moan escaped her lips.

"What were you doing, Nova? You split your skull," Ajax's

question came. The concern in his voice was the opposite of the scolding she expected. The unbearable pain bursting against her skull lifted away as Ajax's magic rushed across her scalp and body. Any wounds she had fused, leaving not even marks of damage.

"I was trying to destroy the dagger," Nova mumbled out. All she could feel was soul crushing defeat for not even being able to use her magic to get rid of her mother's murder weapon.

"Why would you do such a thing? You will need it in your travels," the taller fae scolded her. His arms crossing his chest were the first thing she saw as she cracked her eyes open.

"It killed my mother! I don't want it!" she shouted out, not even caring that the dagger was nowhere nearby. She hoped the burst had sent it to be lost deep within the Feywilds. With a push, she stood with her back against the rough bark of the logs.

"You have my deepest apologies that such a horrific thing has surfaced. If I could change the past, I would have never allowed your mother to be killed," Ajax said, sorrow nestled in his words. She could sense that he blamed himself for what happened as his cold, amethyst gaze softened with regret to match his words. "Nova, I am not fond of being the bearer of this bad news, but that is impossible. The dragon gods cannot even shatter your blade. It is bound to you until your death. It will be yours until your last breath. Were you not aware of this beforehand?"

"No… the memory came while I slept. Until we left the Seelie Court, I barely remembered much of my childhood." Nova couldn't handle Ajax's pitiful stare. Her own eyes turned toward the tree line, finding even then she felt his gaze.

"Those who aren't Seelie find their minds ridden with a fog that keeps your wits and recall dulled. Take the morning easy. You, Shanti, and Alana leave at midday. You will be fine through your journey. I swear my life upon it you can conquer every trial in your path." His lips curled into a devilish smile that she couldn't help but trust. Despite the cruelty described in the myths of the male before her, he'd proven to be someone whose promises she could rely on.

With a rub to her face, she let out an inaudible sigh, thoughts of self-doubt running through her mind, yet through it she felt a fire within burning to make sure she proved Ajax right. "I won't fail you Ajax, after what you've done for me," she stated. If such an awe-inspiring individual saw potential in her, she felt as if she owed him her life.

"I do not make mistakes, Nova. You are more than a plaything for a cruel brat," Ajax stated, each syllable adding weight to her shoulders.

Nova looked to the ground as she pondered his statement, as a wave of exhaustion swept over her. Unable to keep herself standing, she dropped as an ache pulsed through her venom glands and fangs, Ajax's magic catching her in the descent before she crashed into the ground. With a gesture of his hand he had her floating.

She couldn't speak as the fatigue felt like it might be the end of her. Darkness consumed her more than the warmth of Valen's lap surrounding her head, the distant, indecipherable echo of Shanti shouting being the last thing she heard.

Nova sprouted to life, jerking forward with a sharp inhale. Her eyes darted around her surroundings, spotting Alana laid out across the ground asleep first, Ajax and Shanti looming over a map spread out over a small table.

The tap on her shoulder startled her, and as the yelp escaped her lips, her hand clapped over her mouth, her face burning. She snapped her head in the tap's direction, revealing Valen waving at her. "Nova okay?" There was concern written across his face, and an aging expression.

Nova span around, wrapping her arms to the best of her ability around Valen, unable to even touch the tips of her fingers together. "I've been much worse. Just a bad dream and magic accident."

Valen's brow furrowed before he moved to stand, helping Nova to her feet. "Be careful," he suggested.

Nova's empty gut tensed into a tight knot, a familiar ache forming in unison between her belly and venom glands. Her mind raced with thoughts of sinking her teeth into the fleshy neck tucked behind a massive beard. She heard a distant voice calling her name, but it was insignificant compared to her ravenous desires.

Just as she was ready to pounce at the banquet of meat and blood before her, an arm slipped around her throat and locked its hold. "Oi lass, yer a shite vampire," Alana hollered, as her other hand secured both of her wrists. "Ye'd have been on tha wrong end o' Shanti's boot."

"Shame. The day is still young," Shanti said, leaning over to get to Nova's level, delivering a cut on the tip of her nose with a flick. "I'm sure she'll give me three reasons before we stop for camp."

Nova snapped her fangs at Shanti, a sharp hiss following when the tall blonde caught her nose between her fingers. "Lass, calm yer tits!" Alana shifted her hand to pull against her wrist, applying pressure on Nova's throat.

"Cut the shit before I beat you!" Shanti barked out, her grip twisting on Nova's nose enough to draw a howl of pain, with the cartilage being stressed near its limit. Shanti brought her wrist to her own mouth, a quick bite tearing into the flesh. Her iron grip shifted to the mass of blue hair. "Drink. Bite and you will become something's dinner."

Nova stilled against the arm holding her in place. Each drop of blood that fell toward the ground, an individual heartbreak. When the wrist came to her mouth, she pressed her lips over torn flesh, lapping her forked tongue at the blood.

With every gulp, her mind wandered away from the present.

Four paws pounding against the dirt, the healthy prey's odor filled her nose, croaking ravens offering guidance to an elk. Wind rushing against her thick coat with each step. A pure sense of freedom and ferocity swept across her as she darted at the antlered beast. When her jaw snapped around the throat of her next meal, the world slipped away.

Nova opened her eyes, the cravings gone as she felt renewed. There was not a single ache or discomfort as she moved to her feet, noting that she was alone, laid out across the mat she and Valen shared.

Her dagger slung over the end of a stick, with a hand slipped around the sheath fixing it to her waist, she eyed the copper band that, since her eating and recent feeding, fit more snugly around her third finger.

She surveyed the area, seeing no one at their camp. She took off toward the tree Shanti had her striking during training. Standing at the massive trunk, she ran her fingers across the red stained splotch on the bark, lost in contemplation of her recent days.

The rush of heat and wind blew across her face, as a colorful plume of flames crashed into the ground nearby, Valen strutting out as the fiery display ceased. He came to her side, his gruff grin turned sheepish as he brought a hand to the back of his head. "Sorry. Not see Nova."

Nova pulled her hand off the tree and put up her best smile. "You did nothing wrong," she spoke as they began walking toward the camp. "It's our last day together. Do you know how long until I'll see you again?" Nova asked as she stopped to face him, craning her head back to meet his amber eyes.

"Not long. Week. Maybe two?" Valen suggested, a soft touch of his to the small of her back guiding her to keep moving.

Nova pondered the timeframe. Centuries of abuse in comparison seemed shorter than fourteen days without Valen. "Will you be with Ajax when he takes us back to Terra?"

"Yes. Ready for journey?" Valen asked. When she stopped moving, he lifted her into his arms.

The wind tossed her hair as Valen now took full strides instead of little steps to follow her pace. She leaned her head back into his chest. The sound of his heart was a proud, steady beat against her ear. "No, I'm terrified, but if I don't, then no one else will. You said only I'll know how to find my strength..." she stated, biting back the fear tying her stomach in knots.

"Nova strong. Fear good. Bravery conquers fear. Fearless not real." Valen's grin peeked through his messy facial hair.

She matched him with a smile of her own, his words fueling the growing flame in her belly. "Thank you Valen, you're the best male I've ever met!" she announced before running ahead to greet Shanti and Alana as they tidied up the camp.

"About time you got off your ass!" Shanti expressed with ire brimming in her tone. "We have a lot of ground to cover."

Nova gave a nod and moved beside Alana, helping her shut her overstuffed rucksack. "Ye feelin' better, lass?" the brunette asked as she slung her bag across her back.

"Much better! What happened to me?" Nova asked. The experience of losing control, had her wondering if she could regulate herself in the future.

"Ye pushed yerself too hard. Ya need blood, lass. Yer half

vampire, aye? If yer fangs ache, ask me, cannae 'ave ye turnin' feral," Alana answered as she wiped sweat from her brow.

"How often must I feed?" Nova inquired, as Ajax stepped out from a portal not far off to her left.

Alana gave a lazy shrug. "Yer 'alf blooded lass, everythin' about ye will be different."

Nova scowled until Ajax's voice came from behind them. "I have a theory," he mentioned, as the dazzle of his dark red and purple robes caught her eye. "The energy you draw from feeding gets used at greater amounts when you call upon your magic."

"Oh… how do I stop going feral from that?" Nova asked. The idea of being unable to use magic at a whim had her questioning if she could make the journey.

"Learning to cast conservatively will go far. Mind your cravings, feed when needed, and you will be fine," Ajax suggested, a sense of trust shimmering in the dark amethyst abysses that were his eyes. "It's time for you three to leave. Valen and I have a meeting to attend."

Nova paused, having thought she had more time with Valen. "Can we have a couple more hours?" she asked.

"I am afraid not. If I did not need Valen's presence, I would allow it. You have come so far, Nova," Ajax claimed as his hands cupped her cheeks, forcing her to stare into his eyes. "You are the pride and joy of Sela'mann. Show the world that despite her death, she lives on with every breath you draw."

Her eyes grew misty with each syllable he spoke, as his hands against her face summoned a shiver running the length of her spine. The male laid his forehead against hers, an intimate exchange between fae to unite at their mind's eye.

Ajax's tone hushed into a whisper meant only for her ears, as ancient words came from his lips. *"Nova'ivar, I envy your will to live and hope for the future. Raise your voice when others demand your silence."* Both of their eyes shut as she could feel his mana flowing within her, lighting up every single nerve into a beacon, leaving her breathless. *"The fire that burns within you is your greatest asset. Spite those who seek to snuff it by fanning the flames into an inferno."*

Her lips curled into a smile as the inspiring dazzle of Ajax's sincerity settled enough, freeing her from the muted state it had rendered her in.

With a step forward, she wrapped her arms around Ajax. "Thank you, Ajax. I'll have a better way to show how grateful I am when we finish the expedition." When Ajax's arms came around her, she froze in place.

The touch was brief, and when he retracted, so did she. "I trust you will. Say your farewells to Valen," Ajax declared, before a snap of his fingers caused a rift to tear open behind him.

Nova ran toward Valen, throwing her weight at him, the collision with his solid core leaving her dazed. As the fog lifted from her mind, Valen kneeled down to meet Nova at eye level, his embrace sending a series of sharp pops running up her spine, causing her to droop.

"Oi ya lummox yer gon' snap the lass in half!" Alana told Valen as she swatted at his arm.

Nova shot upright and wrapped her arms around Valen, the stress packed deep into her back, pressed out by Valen's hold. She ignored their bickering, even the dull thud of the lycaness sweeping the brunette to the ground.

"You're giving me this kinda hug again soon," Nova breathed out in a weak whisper as Valen had crushed the air from her lungs. "Though I need to breathe…"

When Valen's iron-tight squeeze loosened, she pulled in a sharp inhale before rearing back and giving him a brave smile. "Sorry!" Valen's worried tone came.

"Don't be… I'm strong enough to handle a friendly hug!" Nova replied with a quiet giggle. "I promise."

Valen stood up after giving Nova a kiss to the cheek, all the while placing something made of wood in her hands as he stepped away to follow Ajax into the portal.

Nova's heart felt hollow in this moment, fearful she may never see Valen again. She dreaded this moment, terrified of breaking down and proving that she was too weak for her mother's legacy. Tears stung her eyes as she balled up her fists, staining her nails with blood as they bit deep into her palm.

"Not farewell. See soon," Valen spoke, their gaze interrupted as the rift consumed him.

Nova exhaled a deep breath as the rush of tears ran, no longer able to hold it back. Hands rested on her shoulders, with the strength to snap bones, Alana dug her fingertips into the tense muscles.

"We'll leave when you're ready. Don't take too long or I'm putting my foot up your ass!" Shanti barked out. The maternal quality of her harshness caused Nova to laugh through the tears.

"Fates Shanti…I don't know what I'd do without you," she cleared her tear-stained face with a glimmer of blue magic at the end of her hand after uttering an ancient phrase.

"You'd die," Shanti said, giving Nova a shove, with Alana's hand yanking her away.

"Be nice ta tha lass! She's nae used ta daft adventures," the brunette shouted, throwing her arm around Nova's shoulder.

"Fine. She's not blubbering anymore. We've got fish to fry!" Shanti stated, a snarl rolling out afterward, her foot tapping impatiently.

Nova started walking toward the dense woods of the Feywilds, her eyes drifting to the fading red stain she'd left on the bark of a tree. "Do we have food?" she asked.

"Enough for tonight. Tomorrow we will hunt. You eat what you catch," Shanti spoke as she and Alana flanked Nova, walking beside her. A sensation of security comforted her, knowing she had such awe-inspiring companions to aide her through the journey.

"I've heard stories about the Feywilds… are there deformed fae who would slurp my brain out of my nose?" Nova asked.

"Deformed? Most are just ugly," Shanti replied, scaling the

side of a tree as they entered the Feywilds.

"Maybe a few arse hats're inta' tha kinna shenanigans. Dinnae ever eat tha fungus. Yer better bein' hungry if're unsure, aye?" Alana said, walking right into a low hanging tree and falling onto her ass. "Oi! Fack these trees!"

Nova stopped to help Alana up as Shanti hung from a branch, her blonde hair getting into her eyes. "Can you not? I don't enjoy pissing off the trees," Shanti uttered a frustrated sigh.

"Thank ya, lass!" Alana spoke as she took Nova's hand and pulled herself up, shoving Shanti's hair out of the way. "Ignore tha cranky bitch."

Nova scowled and shook her head. "Are you okay?" she asked as she eyed the path ahead, looking for low-hanging branches and trip hazards.

"Aye nae anythin' new," Alana said as she followed behind Nova. "Ye see a safe route, lass?"

"Yes! I didn't know you were clumsy?" Nova asked as she led the brunette to weave through the trees.

Alana snorted in amusement before speaking. "Am used ta' rollin' hills nae tha woods shite!"

"Being a boozehound rotted her brain into slop," Shanti said, the sound of her boots smacking into branches ringing out, as she ran ahead of them in the colorful natural canopy above their heads.

"Yer right, ye mangey bitch! Least'm nae a walking flea inn!" Alana snapped back.

Nova laughed at the two of them. She enjoyed their crass bond. She idolized Shanti and Alana. "Do you two love to fight?"

"Aye! Keeps ya on yer toes, ready fer anythin'. Ye'll get there, lass," Alana said.

Shanti dropped several strides ahead of Nova, her clenched fist held upright. She came to an abrupt halt as Shanti pressed her ear to the tree. "We move west, there's a sphinx blocking the route to the north. Fucker moved."

"Can't we fight it?" Nova asked, as she stepped close to Shanti.

"Waste of time. Only way to deal with them is to solve riddles," Shanti said as she began walking to the west. "I fucking hate riddles!"

Nova's brow furrowed in confusion as she followed every step Shanti took. "You can talk to trees?"

"My *Volva* taught me, not all trees are what they seem." Shanti said.

"Long as we're nae dealin' wit' psions! Hate those shites proddin' at me, noodle!" Alana snarled out and poked at her own scalp aggressively.

Nova laughed at Alana's emphatic behavior. "That sounds scary!"

"It is not as if you can pop their eyes with your fingers. Psions need to see you," Shanti explained while gouging the air with her fingers shaped in a V.

Nova shuddered at the idea of bursting something's eyes

with her fingers. "That's barbaric!" she said, trying to prevent fear from consuming her.

"A warrior with a shovel is better than a gardener with a dagger, you'll get it after a war or two." Shanti said, with a raise of her fist again. "North now. There's a faint scent of a basilisk to the west. Alana always gets turned to stone when we fight one."

"How will I wind up in a war?" Nova hadn't expected that her freedom meant war.

Alana bumped into Nova's back as she was taking a deep pull from one of her bottles. "Yer pals wit' us an' Ajax. We're always in tha middle of whatever strife is ravagin' tha' world!"

"Fates… aren't you worried about dying?" Nova asked as she ducked beneath a branch.

"No point in living if death is far away. Don't be fucking soft!" Shanti said as she halted the trio again with her raised fist and a turn of her head with her finger to her lips.

Several silent moments passed before a foot the width of Valen's wingspan crashed down in front of them, smashing trees into the ground.

Nova craned her eyes up to see a male looking creature, bald with minimal clothes and only a scraggly beard dangling from its face. The massive being even had a log slung over its shoulder.

The trio waited as the giant kept going until it was out of sight. With an anxious exhale, Nova felt relieved. "I thought the giants all died?" she said in a nervous whisper.

"Nae lass, just a few left. Bes' ta lettem pass," Alana said as they continued their path ahead.

"Keep an eye out for somewhere to set up camp. I'd rather stop before it gets dark. Nova, I'm only telling you this once. You don't wander from camp! If you can't feel the fire, you're too far," Shanti's warning came, striking a sense of panic in her, terrified to disobey her wisdom.

"Okay… how do I tell a suitable spot to camp?" Nova asked, receiving a lecture from Shanti of different ways to pick camps.

Frazzled from the unloading of knowledge, Nova followed behind Shanti, as the trio moved in silence, until Alana burst out hours later as she discovered an alcove of stones that made for adequate shelter.

www.ingramcontent.com/pod-product-compliance
Lightning Source LLC
Chambersburg PA
CBHW020801310726
48969CB00002B/646